The Gingerbread Girls

Coming together in time for Christmas

The Gingerbread Inn is where best friends Emily, Andrea and Casey spent much of their childhood. Now all grown-up, they're back—older, wiser, but still with as much need of a little Massachusetts magic as ever. As Christmas approaches, and three gorgeous men appear on the scene, is it time to create some new treasured memories?

Don't miss

HER SECRET LITTLE BABY BUMP
by Shirley Jump in October 2013

MARRY ME UNDER THE MISTLETOE
by Rebecca Winters in November 2013

And SNOWFLAKES AND SILVER LININGS
by Cara Colter in December 2013

Dear Reader,

I met my best friend when I was ten. We're still best friends. When we were young we used to go to her cabin in Brighton, Utah, and spend many summer and winter nights up there in the mountains. We shared thoughts and dreams that have now come to pass, and of course there's so much more coming in the future.

When I was asked to write the second novel in this Christmas series about three best friends, I thought immediately of those wonderful days with my own dear friend in that cabin that spelled magic for me. It was easy to imagine my heroine Andrea staying at the Gingerbread Inn with the man of her dreams. But they have some obstacles to overcome, of course. The path to true love has its rocky moments....

I hope you'll find magic in this love story.

Enjoy!

Rebecca Winters

Marry Me under the Mistletoe

Rebecca Winters

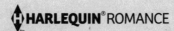

HARLEQUIN® ROMANCE

Recycling programs
for this product may
not exist in your area.

ISBN-13: 978-0-373-74267-7

MARRY ME UNDER THE MISTLETOE

First North American Publication 2013

Copyright © 2013 by Rebecca Winters

Printed in U.S.A.

HARLEQUIN®
www.Harlequin.com

Rebecca Winters, whose family of four children has now swelled to include five beautiful grandchildren, lives in Salt Lake City, Utah, in the land of the Rocky Mountains. With canyons and high alpine meadows full of wildflowers, she never runs out of places to explore. They, plus her favorite vacation spots in Europe, often end up as backgrounds for her romance novels, because writing is her passion, along with her family and church.

Rebecca loves to hear from readers. If you wish to email her, please visit her website, www.cleanromances.com.

Recent books by Rebecca Winters

A MARRIAGE MADE IN ITALY
ALONG CAME TWINS... *
BABY OUT OF THE BLUE *
THE COUNT'S CHRISTMAS BABY
THE RANCHER'S HOUSEKEEPER
A BRIDE FOR THE ISLAND PRINCE
SNOWBOUND WITH HER HERO

Tiny Miracles

Other titles by this author available in ebook format at www.Harlequin.com.

To Lib.

What would our youth have been like without each other?
I don't even want to think about it.

CHAPTER ONE

JUST TWO WEEKS until Christmas and so-o much to do.

The latest merchandise from suppliers needed to be put in the window. The Hansel and Gretel shop located on Lemon Street in downtown Providence, Rhode Island, was a favorite place all year long for customers wanting imported hand-painted wooden gifts, nutcrackers, little girls' Bavarian dirndls and little boys' Tyrolean hats. But especially at Christmas.

Andrea Fleming finished her morning coffee, then quickly dressed in a navy wool skirt and a long-sleeved navy pullover with Snoopy on the front wearing a Santa's hat. After running a brush through her shoulder-length gilt-blond hair, she slipped into her comfortable wedgies and hurried downstairs to the shop below.

She'd been living here since her husband's death fourteen months ago. They'd been married only three weeks and had been staying with his parents in Braunschweig, Germany, when they'd been in a car accident and he was killed outright. She'd survived, but had been forced to stay in hospital following an operation.

Her mother had been there to help her recover enough so that she could board a plane. When she returned home it was without her husband and no hope of ever having children.

Though her divorced mom wanted Andrea to live at home with her, she'd preferred to renovate the loft above the shop so she could stay there. She felt closer to Gunter somehow in the store she'd always felt was enchanted.

She'd been twenty-three when he'd first brought merchandise to her family's store in place of his father. His grandparents were the original creators of the world-famous Braunschweig nutcrackers and wooden pyramids. His dark blond good looks and blue eyes had captivated her and they'd fallen in love. Within the year they were married.

They'd had a wedding reception here in Providence with all her family and friends. His family had held another one for them in Germany. It had been a picture-perfect wedding for both sets of families.

No one could have foreseen the crash that took Andrea's husband. In one moment she'd lost him as well as her ability to conceive. Never would she have a child with him. Never would she have a child of her own body. A sob escaped her.

Don't dwell on that right now, Andrea.

After checking the thermostat to make sure the shop was warm enough, she walked out back to start unpacking the boxes from their suppliers that had arrived yesterday afternoon. In the first one she discovered an exquisitely made Braunschweig wooden rocking chair and put the price tag on it.

Without hesitation she carried it through the shop to the window and set it next to the decorated Christmas tree that was part of the Santa's workshop display. The chair needed something special. She had dozens of dolls, floppy elves and Christmas angels. Any one of them would look cute sitting in it. She would have to think about it while she finished unpacking.

"Oh!" she cried when she opened the last box and found a three-foot-tall gingerbread boy. It was made of dark chocolate-colored dotted Swiss fabric. A red, green and gold plaid ribbon was tied around his neck at a jaunty angle with a little golden bell hanging down.

He had large, shiny blue buttons for eyes, round pink felt cheeks and an impish smiley mouth done in red ribbon as if to say, "You can run and run as fast as you can, but you can't catch me. I'm the gingerbread man." The body was outlined in white bric-a-brac trim.

"You're so perfect I can't believe it!" She attached the price tag to it. "If Gunter hadn't had that accident, we'd have a little boy or girl who would love you as much as I do." Tears stung her eyes as sorrow overwhelmed her.

Surrounded by many items meant for a child, she knew this shop was a constant reminder of her loss. But the store was also a family treasure and legacy she loved, and of course there was the comfort and joy of working alongside her mother, who'd done everything to help her overcome her grief.

Andrea thought she'd been doing a little better, but for some reason this gingerbread man spoke to her inner heart. It was at bittersweet times like this that she had to fight against succumbing to the terrible pain of knowing she'd never have her own baby.

Though her mom gently reminded her that one day she'd meet another man and there was always adoption, Andrea couldn't imagine it. What man, when given a choice, would want an infertile widow?

After hugging the gingerbread man to her chest until the painful moment passed, she walked over to the window and placed it in the new chair. Once she'd added the latest set of nutcrackers from the Bavarian kings collection to the others, she flipped the switch on the wall and the window display came alive with colored lights and sounds.

On the floor around the tree loaded with wooden ornaments she'd placed an animated elf band with drums, cymbals and horns. Children and adults alike always stopped to watch their antics. Usually it brought people inside to buy an identical set and they ended up going home with more gifts.

On impulse she pulled the smartphone from her pocket and stepped inside the display area to take a couple of pictures. Wait till she sent them to the gingerbread girls. That was the nickname for her and her best friends Emily and Casey. Recently they'd lost Melissa, the other member of their special group.

They'd all met years ago on summer vacation at the Gingerbread Inn in Massachusetts and the nickname had stuck. Their families had continued to meet there every summer and the girls had become fast friends, a bond that had lasted to this day. But with Melissa gone, Andrea couldn't handle any more sadness thinking about that.

Instead she concentrated on getting the small shop ready for customers. Her mom would be over later in the day to help. Throughout the holidays Andrea opened up at nine-thirty rather than ten, and closed at eight rather than six. It was almost opening time now.

She ran the vacuum over the carpet and watered the pots of red poinsettias placed around the room among all the wooden objects displayed. The thoughtful manager of the floral shop next door had sent a centerpiece featuring white Asiatic lilies and red roses. Andrea set it on the counter. With the profusion of lights and decorations, she had to admit it looked like a fairyland.

Before she unlocked the front door, she went into the office in back and checked her emails on the computer. To her astonishment she saw a message from gingerbread3. That was Casey Caravetta's user name. Since Andrea was the youngest, her email was gingerbread4, Emily was 1, and Melissa's had been 2.

What a coincidence! She'd just been thinking about her friends. Andrea prayed this was good news, the kind she wanted to hear from Casey, who'd lived through a broken engagement a year ago and was still down from it. Andrea opened the message.

Hey, Andrea, it's moi. Could you possibly drop things and drive over to the Gingerbread Inn today? I've got to talk to you.

Oh, no. Things didn't sound any better for Casey since the last time they'd talked.

One of my issues is I'm up in the air about Christmas and the problems with my family (as always).

Casey was at the inn now? In winter?

I came to our favorite place because it seemed to work such magic for Emily, but I can't believe what it's like here. You should see how run-down it is. I could cry.

The three of them had suffered thinking of it gradually deteriorating.

As you know, Carol's always been like a mother to all of us and is taking great care of me. She's such a sweetheart. So's Harper, who lies at my feet and looks up at me with those soulful puppy eyes.

Warm memories of bygone days flooded Andrea. Throughout their youth they'd had marvelous times together with no hint of what lay in store for them beyond the horizon of Barrow's Lake.

I'd give anything if you'd join me. You're not that far away from Barrow's Cove. I realize how busy you are at the shop this time of year, but I need you and your wisdom, especially after what you've been through.

Andrea didn't have any wisdom. She was an empty vessel.

Let me know if you can make it, even if it's only for one night. Remember when we talked about giving a party at the inn on Christmas Eve so Emily and Cole can renew their wedding vows? This would be the perfect time to formalize our plans. So see what you can do to get away.

Love ya, Casey.

Andrea closed the message and left the office to open the door to the shop. She glanced at the Advent calendar hanging on the wall, one of several dozen with chocolate tokens in each window. Luckily it was Wednesday—not the weekend, which was their busiest time.

The inn on Barrow's Lake outside Barrow's Cove, Massachusetts, was only an hour away from Providence. If she left after her mother came over, she could spend the night with Casey and drive home tomorrow in time to relieve her mom by afternoon.

She checked the weather app on her phone. No new storm systems right now. Though they'd had snow in the Northeast, most of the main roads had been plowed. It wouldn't take any time to pack for one overnight.

Andrea had already decided which nut-crackers she would give her friends for Christmas. All she had to do was wrap them and take them with her. She could give them out at the party on Christmas Eve.

During her musings an elderly gentle-man walked into the store. It activated some Christmas chimes. When he said he wanted to browse, she used that time to phone her mom. As soon as she told her about the email, her mom told her to go for several days if she wanted, accusing her of never taking a vacation.

Andrea loved her mother, but told her she needed only one night. In truth she didn't like being away from the shop. It kept her going. Too much free time and she started to think about things that dragged her down to despair. None of that this year!

She got back on the computer and sent

Casey a message that she was coming. Then she gift wrapped a smoker for her customer. After taking his credit card information, she handed him his package. That was when she saw a tall, striking male, maybe thirty-ish, standing outside the window wearing a bomber jacket. He was carrying a blonde girl of five or six in his arms so she could see everything.

Loving the girl's animation, Andrea walked over to the window to watch. The child was pointing at the gingerbread boy, her face and eyes beguiled by him. Closer now, Andrea could see she wore a pink parka with a hood lined in fur. It had fallen back to reveal her soft golden curls that fell to her shoulders.

Against the bright pink color, the man's short cropped jet-black hair stood out. With brows the same color, he was darkly attractive. His lean chiseled jaw had that five-o'clock shadow that looked good only on a certain type of male.

When the little girl laughed at the antics of the drummer elf, the lines of his hard mouth broke into a half smile, causing Andrea's breath to catch. She had the strongest suspicion he didn't laugh often. Suddenly his gaze shifted to Andrea's, as if he could read her mind and didn't like it.

Completely embarrassed and shaken to be caught staring at him, she walked back to the counter. That was the first time anything like that had happened since Gunter's death. There'd been plenty of attractive men coming in and out of the shop since her return from Germany, but they weren't in this man's class.

A second later she heard the chimes again before the charismatic man approached her. The girl walked at his side, clinging to his hand. With those light green eyes, they had to be father and daughter, although his were more hazel in color and a deeper hue.

"Good morning. May I help you?"

"I hope so," Rick Jenner said to the blonde saleswoman. "Do you have a set of animated elves like the one in the window?"

"Right over here on this table." She walked to it and picked up a box.

When she put it on the counter, his daughter stared at him with imploring eyes. "Will you ask her if I can hold the gingerbread man, Daddy?"

"No, Tessa. It's too expensive."

"What's expensive?"

"It costs too much," he said and pulled the credit card from his wallet to pay for the elves.

"I wish I could look at it." Tears welled in her eyes. If he had a dollar for every time she wished she could have something…

The clerk ringing up the sale took one look at those eyes and said, "Stay right there and I'll bring it to you." After handing him back his card and purchase, she walked around the counter and hurried over to the display window to pluck the gingerbread man and rocking chair from the case.

Good grief. His daughter was a little manipulator, a talent she'd learned from his deceased wife, who'd been indulged in turn by her own well-meaning parents, especially her mother, Nancy. He'd loved his wife and they'd had a good marriage, but she'd been high maintenance, which had caused minor strains and at times a few major ones. Rick was determined his daughter would learn she couldn't have everything she wanted.

When the clerk walked over to them, he became aware of her enticing fragrance, a light floral one. "If you'll sit down, you can hold him."

Rick wished she hadn't gone to the trouble, but it was too late now.

"Oh—" Tessa crooned after taking it in her arms. His daughter's happiness almost blinded him. "He's so cute." In a perfectly natural gesture, she kissed the cheeks just the way a mother would kiss her baby. Then she held it tight and with eyes closed started rocking.

The sight caused Rick's throat to swell. He was in luck. Only the first day of shopping to get an idea of what Tessa wanted and already he knew *this* would be the present Santa left under the tree. When he got home, he would ask his housekeeper to come in and buy it for him so it could be a surprise.

"We have to leave now, Tessa. We've got more shopping to do before I take you to kindergarten. Thank the nice lady for letting you hold him."

Tessa stared at the saleswoman. "Thank you."

"You're welcome."

He helped her off the chair and set the gingerbread man inside it.

Tessa's lower lip trembled. "Can't I have him, Daddy?"

"I'm afraid not."

"Please?"

"Tessa—that's enough."

"I'll sell it to you at half price," the woman said under her breath. He lifted his head and found himself gazing into the sapphire-blue eyes that had unexpectedly caught his attention through the display window.

"Thank you, but no."

On cue his daughter broke into tears. The clerk bent over her. "Have you written to Santa Claus yet?"

"Yes. My grandma helped me, b-but I didn't ask for the gingerbread man." Her voice wobbled.

"I'm sure your father will help you write another letter and ask Santa to bring you a gingerbread man." She flicked him a hopeful glance as she said it.

"This one?" Tessa pointed to the chair.

"Yes."

Rick blinked. *Yes?* The clerk's no doubt well-meaning intervention irritated the hell out of him. Worse, she'd played right into his daughter's hands.

Tessa sniffed. "Do you think Santa will know that my gingerbread man is in this store?"

An impish smile broke the corner of the clerk's mouth, drawing his unwilling attention to its provocative shape. "Yes."

"Promise?"

"I promise."

"Come on, Tessa." He picked up his daughter, who still wasn't in control of her tears.

"Have a merry Christmas!" The woman just kept it up.

Rick flashed her a brief glance. "Merry Christmas. Thank you for indulging her." With his daughter in one arm and his package in the other, he left the shop in a few long, swift strides.

Was that a little sarcasm Andrea had heard?

She bristled, realizing that he hadn't wanted his daughter indulged and didn't appreciate in the least what Andrea had done.

But maybe he couldn't afford it because he was out of work. He *had* told his daughter it cost too much. If that was the case, then she felt bad for putting him on the spot, and she decided she would grant his little girl her wish by Christmas.

Andrea knew exactly where to send the gingerbread man and the chair. The credit card listed him as Richard Jenner on Rose Drive in Elmhurst, a nice neighborhood. It was Christmas, a time for giving.

This could be her own little sub-for-Santa project. Every year at the church they had a list of families who needed help, and everyone who could contribute did so. This was one time when Andrea knew her present would bring happiness.

Picking up one of the big floppy elves, she took him over by the tree and put him in place of the gingerbread man and the rocker. Those items she took up the back stairs to the loft. Once she got everything gift wrapped and packed, then she'd send it to the Jenner residence. On the outside of the box she'd print "To Tessa from Santa."

With that accomplished she went back downstairs to face a steady stream of customers until her mother arrived so she could leave for Barrow's Lake.

During the late-afternoon drive her mind played over the incident in the store. What she'd give to have a child she could indulge. With those cherubic features, Tessa Jenner was absolutely adorable.

When she reached the Gingerbread Inn, she saw the state it was in and realized that Casey's email hadn't exaggerated. Despite some cosmetic fix-ups by Emily and her husband, Cole Watson, it was obvious the Gingerbread Inn had fallen on hard times. Despite all the inn owner's big dreams, Carol Parsons had lost her husband and couldn't keep everything going anymore.

In the kitchen, the heart of the once-fabulous two-story Georgian inn, Andrea looked around. Everything needed refurbishing. She longed to get rid of the dilapidated sunflower wallpaper and worn white vinyl flooring and make it all fresh again.

But Andrea was grateful for one thing that hadn't changed. She and Casey, her exotic-looking friend with the dark wild hair, were sitting at the very same long maple table where the girls had enjoyed many a meal day or night in past summers.

"Do you two want another cup of cocoa?"

Andrea jumped up from the chair and gave Carol another hug. The tiny gray-haired widow and sole owner was in her fifties and still looked great wearing a pale blue T-shirt and jeans. Best of all, she had a heart as big as the outdoors.

To the amusement of all, Harper, the golden retriever of uncertain mix, ran around sniffing everyone, hoping for crumbs from Carol's homemade coffee cake fresh from the oven.

"Don't you know you've done enough? It's after midnight. You should be in bed. Casey and I will be headed there ourselves pretty soon."

"No, you won't." She laughed. "I know you girls. Once you get talking, there's no stopping you. Since you have to get back to Providence tomorrow, I'm going to leave you two alone so you can catch up. In the morning I'll make scones."

"Those are to die for," the girls said in a collective voice.

Carol laughed. "Come on, Harper." The dog made a yapping sound and scrambled out the door after her.

Andrea and Casey were finally alone, surrounded by six empty chairs. One of them would never see Melissa again. Once upon a time they'd been filled with people and laughter and great happiness. Andrea wondered if she'd ever know real happiness again. Her hurt went so deep she couldn't fathom experiencing it again, let alone joy.

Casey studied her for a minute through dark brown eyes. "I know what you're thinking."

Andrea nodded. "Life has changed for all of us. Remember that horrid expression, 'Life is what happens when you had other plans'?"

"Oh, yeah. I could have written it."

"I think Eve probably coined the expression," Andrea murmured.

"Except I think things might be changing for Carol."

"Really?"

She smiled. "Cole hired a handyman to help around here. His name is Martin Johnson. He's been a widower for ten years and from what I can tell, he and Carol are getting along better than you'd believe. Having been a carpenter, he can fix anything."

"What's he like?"

"Tall and blue-eyed with the greatest shock of white hair."

"Wouldn't it be something if a romance blossomed around here?"

Casey nodded as they stared at each other for a long serious moment. "It's so good to see you and I'm so-o glad you came. I'm feeling alone and maybe more than a tad envious of Emily, who's off on her second honeymoon with Cole."

"I feel the same way, so let's get busy planning what we're going to do with this place to turn it into a winter wonderland for their vow-renewal ceremony."

Once they'd worked it all out Andrea said, "Tell me what's hanging so heavily on you right now."

"Oh, Andrea, I just feel like I don't want to be filled with self-pity around you when you've experienced so much loss. I guess I hoped to recapture some of that girlish wonder we had for so many years. But we can't turn back the clock. When I think about you and Gunter…I don't know how you're dealing with your life. It's all so unfair."

Andrea had known this conversation would leap to her own problems. "Let's agree the word *fair* should be stricken from the language. Luckily his parents have three other children and four grandchildren to dote on, and I have my mom and the shop."

"I'm glad about that. I know how much work is saving your life right now. But forgive me for asking another question. How will you ever move on if everywhere you turn, you see him?"

A weary sigh escaped her lips. "Mom has begged me to move back to the house with her for that very reason, but I'm not ready yet and don't know if I ever will be. She belongs to a church group that meets every few weeks. There's a widower I know she's interested in, but he's been on vacation. I'm hoping that when he gets back, he'll sweep her off her feet. If I'm not living there, it'll make his path easier."

"I love your mom. Any man would be lucky to find a woman like her. But I want to see you fall in love like that again."

"The chances against that happening are astronomical, Casey."

"Surely not. I predict some gorgeous guy is going to come along and you won't know what hit you. Maybe this fantastic man will see you in the shop and find you absolutely irresistible the way Gunter did."

"Maybe."

Heat rushed into her cheeks as a vision of Tessa's father filled her mind. He *was* fantastic looking, but if anything, she knew he'd felt like swatting her away from him rather than sweeping her off her feet. The encounter had disturbed her more than she wanted to admit.

Mr. Jenner had a daughter, for heaven's sake. Though he didn't wear a wedding ring—Andrea blushed to realize she had noticed—he was probably in an intimate relationship with a woman, so there was no point in wasting energy discussing him. The last person he'd be interested in was a widow who couldn't give a man more children.

Though she was tempted to tell Casey about the incident, she held back, needing to concentrate on anything that didn't have to do with the ache inside her. Andrea had her sister-in-law when she really needed to talk. With Marie she could open up. She'd been there right after the accident. They'd become close after Andrea had met Gunter, and they needed each other now that he was gone so they could mourn together.

"It has to happen one day, Andrea. You're too young and beautiful."

"And unable to conceive, don't forget."

"There's always adoption."

"That's what Mom says, but it's ludicrous to go there. I just don't want to think about it."

"Understood."

Feeling at a complete loose end, Andrea got to her feet and did the dishes. Once the kitchen was cleaned up, she took a deep breath. "You know what? It's late. Why don't we go to bed, and tomorrow we'll get up and drink hot chocolate, take a walk to the lake and think about Emily and Cole having a baby and how wonderful life can be. I've never been here in the snow."

"Nor I. If circumstances were different for you and me, this could be a very romantic winter getaway."

"*If* being the operative word," Andrea added wryly to cover her troubled emotions.

At least their plans for the wedding-renewal vows on Christmas Eve had been made. But much as she was thrilled to see Casey and leave the nutcrackers for everyone, their conversation had opened up her wounds and she was bleeding all over the place. This bleakness in her heart threatened to overwhelm her. She needed to get back to work where she wouldn't think. "Casey—"

"I know what you're going to say," Casey interrupted. They read each other's minds quite easily. "You're restless as a cat wanting out of a cage."

"The inn is hardly a cage."

"It is when you're needing other things to occupy your mind. Go on back to Providence after breakfast. To be honest, I'm afraid I'm suffering from the same problem. I'll probably head back when you do. I've got a project going for Emily's baby on my quilting frame at home. I'm making her a special quilt with a picture of the Gingerbread Inn in the center."

"Oh, how darling!" Andrea cried. "You've just given me an idea for a gift that will look perfect in her nursery." When more rocking chairs and gingerbread men arrived, she'd put a set away for Emily. On the way back to Providence, she'd put in a big order for both items.

In her mind's eye Andrea kept remembering Tessa rocking back and forth with her prize in her arms.... Oh, how she'd love to see that precious girl on Christmas morning when she ran to find out what Santa had brought her. To give birth to a daughter like Tessa Jenner would be joy beyond measure. But it wasn't meant to be. The sooner she got that child off her mind, the better.

She turned out the lights and they went up to bed. Clearly Casey was in so much turmoil herself, she didn't press Andrea to stay longer. They'd said all there was to say for the time being. Now they both needed their own caves to lick their wounds while they struggled to survive.

CHAPTER TWO

"LADDER 1 RESPOND to art-gallery fire on Lemon Street and Sixth."

The dispatcher's voice over the gong galvanized everyone into action. Hearing the address, Rick felt his adrenaline kick in. *Lemon Street?* After parking his car, he'd walked by that gallery earlier in the morning with Tessa. Only a florist shop separated it from the Hansel and Gretel shop.

He didn't plan to go there again and had planned to send his housekeeper to buy the gingerbread man for him. Not only did he have time constraints, he preferred to avoid a good-looking woman like the salesclerk who wore no ring. After losing his wife, he wanted to spare himself and Tessa that kind of pain ever again. Another romantic relationship was out of the question for him.

Unfortunately if the fire spread, that shop's inventory, including the gingerbread man, might go up in smoke before the night was over. The clock said 9:55 p.m. Hopefully the woman had long since gone home from work. He broke out in a cold sweat just thinking about her getting overcome by fumes or worse. Rick knew firsthand what that was like; as a child he'd almost died in a fire. That experience had changed the direction of his life.

"Let's go!" he called to his crew as he grabbed his turnout gear and headed for the engine. Arney drove them out of the truck bay to the downtown area. Rick got on the phone to the battalion chief discussing methods to proceed when he saw smoke pouring out of the third-story window of the art gallery. Engine 2 was first in, but the alarm had sounded for more help.

"Mel? You work with Arney. Jose? You're with me." Out of the corner of his eye Rick saw another ladder truck pull up to the fire ground. Already a couple of men from the engine truck had gone into the building with the hoses.

"Ready, Jose?"

He gave the sign and together they placed the ladder in an alley that gave access to the building and set it against the wall. After putting on their masks, they ascended. Their job was to hunt for any injured or unconscious people trapped in there.

The smoke continued to pour out the third-story window. Everything was black by the time he climbed inside the frame where the glass had blown out. Ladder 2 down the alley was having trouble opening up the side of the building to ventilate. The smoke was really heavy now. Rick's intuition was that the hoses had extinguished most of the fire and what was left was smoke from the burned electrical insulation.

He and Jose crawled in on their bellies, but after a few minutes of going from room to room, they were satisfied no one was inside except the fire crews. The smoke started to be drawn off, which meant the ventilation was finally working.

Dozens of charred canvases lay in heaps in one of the rooms on the top floor. Something about the arrangement of them didn't look right—strange even. He had a gut feeling the fire had been started there on purpose. After more probing he knew they had to have been placed in a pile like that.

When he got back to the station he would tell Benton Ames, the head of the arson squad and Rick's best friend. After more inspection, he made his way down the watery, debris-filled stairway.

Once outside, he pulled off his mask. Thank goodness the fire hadn't spread. It had mostly been contained on the third floor. The Hansel and Gretel shop was still standing. With a sense of relief that both it and the florist shop had been spared, he helped Jose bring down the extension. Soon they'd done their cleanup, and they rode back to the station. His ten-hour shift was at an end and he could go home.

The battalion chief got him on the phone. "When you report to the station tomorrow, take the truck to Lemon Street on your way to training exercises. I want you and your crew to talk to the businesses on either side and across from the art gallery. Get a report if they sustained any smoke damage of significance."

Another rush of adrenaline charged his body. That meant he might be seeing *her* again. Just the thought of it raised his blood pressure. Somehow her appeal had slipped past his defenses. He couldn't figure it out.

"Yes, sir."

Fifteen minutes later he pulled into the driveway of his house and let himself in the front door. Sharon Milne, his live-in house-keeper, would have put Tessa to bed at eight-thirty. His daughter had made him promise he'd help her write a letter to Santa in the morning.

Rick went to the kitchen and drank from the tap until he'd quenched his thirst, then he headed for his bedroom. After a shower and shave, he put on a robe and walked down the hall to Tessa's room.

He tiptoed inside and sat on the side of the bed to look at her. In sleep her profile re-minded him a lot of his deceased wife, Tina. She'd been gone a year. They'd lost her to leukemia a month before Christmas after a year's fight against the disease. This was the hardest time for both of them.

Tessa had been very upset with him when he'd dropped her off at kindergarten today. She'd wanted to know why they couldn't go back and get the gingerbread man.

There'd been several reasons. Once again Rick had given her another talk about being grateful for the things she had and not to expect to be appeased at every turn. After Tina's death he'd done his share of giving their daughter things to comfort her in their grief, but it hadn't taken long before he'd realized it was the wrong thing to do.

She expected everyone to satisfy her slightest wish. His wife and her family had done too much of that in the past. Before Tina's passing, Tessa had already felt entitled. He smoothed the blond hair off her forehead. Rick didn't want his daughter growing up with a princess complex.

But there was more bothering him. How could he explain to a five-year-old how he'd felt when he saw the clerk looking at him through the shop window with those brilliant blue eyes? She was the kind of woman the guys at the station would call a real stunner—blonde and curvaceous with classic features. Most likely she was married with children. Her response to Tessa had seemed very natural. It meant his thoughts should stop right there. The absence of a wedding ring didn't always prove anything.

Rick had felt dead inside for so long, he was shocked to discover he could have an emotional response to the looks of a beautiful woman again. The psychiatrist provided by the department had talked to him at length about dealing with his grief. He'd told Rick that one day he'd start to feel alive again, but there was no set time when it would happen.

Rick certainly hadn't expected the first signs of it to happen this morning. Part of the anger he'd felt masked guilt, because it seemed as if he was being disloyal to Tina even to notice another woman so soon after her death. The psychiatrist had warned him about that, too. He'd said it was perfectly natural to feel guilt, and he might feel it for a long time. If it went on too long, however, then he wanted to see him back in his office.

After the clerk had waited on him, his anger had grown worse because she'd been so incredibly nice and tuned in to Tessa's feelings. He didn't want her doing either of them any favors. For one thing, Tessa was *his* daughter.

The woman obviously thought he didn't have enough money to pay for the gingerbread man, so she'd lowered the price. He had to admit it had injured his pride. But after having a whole day to think about it, he recognized what he'd really been feeling.

The last thing he wanted was to feel beholden to her or any woman. Sharon, the housekeeper, was different in her caretaker role.

Face it, Jenner. You resent being attracted to her.

That was the truth of it. He supposed the fact that she was the first person since Tina's death to take his mind off his wife for a few minutes made him feel vulnerable. But for her to play Santa hadn't sat well with him. So many emotions had bombarded him, he hadn't been able to get out of the shop fast enough.

No one could take Tina's place as Tessa's mother. He couldn't trust another woman with that job. Rick didn't want another woman in his life. He didn't want to have those kinds of feelings ever again. It had hurt so much to lose Tina. He couldn't live through pain like that a second time. Once was enough for him and Tessa. He'd do whatever he could to protect both of them from more suffering.

Frustrated as hell because he would have to go by her business tomorrow, he leaned over to kiss his daughter's forehead before leaving to go to his own room. Maybe he'd get one of the crew to do it. Either way, it would be a short visit and that would be the end of it.

Before he went to bed he made a detour to the living room and set up the elf band beneath the Christmas tree they'd bought and decorated last night. When Tessa got up in the morning, she'd run in here to find out what the noise was and be delighted.

Now, if he could just get the woman out of his head so he could go to sleep… But that was a joke, because she'd been flitting through his mind—all the amazing parts of her, starting with her smile and the way her blue eyes shimmered.

At ten the next morning Arney pulled the fire truck in front of the scarred top half of the art gallery. An inspection team from the arson squad was walking around.

When Rick saw Benton, he climbed down from the truck in his gear and walked over to his sandy-haired friend. He and his wife, Deanna, an attractive brunette, had two children, one of whom was Tessa's friend Julie at kindergarten. They'd all become close during Tina's illness.

Benton patted him on the shoulder. "Thanks to your tip, we know this is the work of the same arsonist who started that department-store blaze three weeks ago. Underneath that pile of canvases, he'd filled a plastic milk carton with gasoline and made a wick with a piece of shirt. It was a slow burner, but did enough damage to ignite the whole thing."

"He probably used the fire escape here to knock out that third-story window we climbed into. I thought it had been blown out by the fire."

"Let's hope he's caught soon. In the meantime I've spoken to the police chief. They're going to keep this downtown area under heavy surveillance 24/7 until after the holidays."

"That's good." If Benton hadn't mentioned it, Rick would have.

"How's it going?"

Rick didn't have to pretend around him. "Don't ask."

"That's what I thought. Deanna and I are having a little party on Saturday night. We want you to come. Susie Anderson from Engine 3 will be coming along with some of the others. She specifically asked if you'd be there." He put his hand up. "I know what you're going to say about that, but at least promise me you'll think about it."

"Susie's a good firefighter and nice in her own way, but she's been a part of the landscape for too long a time. She's just one of the guys to me, Benton. Everyone's been trying to line me up, but I just can't do it. I don't feel the spark. Without that…"

"Then bring a friend, so Susie won't get any ideas. If it's your housekeeper's night off, then bring Tessa. She and Julie can play."

Rick was aware the guys were waiting for him. He turned to his crew, having made a certain decision. "Mel? You and Arney cover the florist and the Hansel and Gretel shop. Jose? Go talk to the cleaners across the street. I'll take the print shop."

Once the men took off, he eyed Benton and gave him a clap on the shoulder. "Thanks for the invite. I promise I'll think about it."

His friend winked. "Good."

Before Rick walked across the street, his gaze wandered to the display window of the shop. Yesterday he'd looked into a pair of blue eyes in an angel face with a golden halo of hair. It had felt as if a thunderbolt had passed through him.

But neither the gingerbread man nor the little rocking chair was there now. That meant she'd pulled the items after he'd left the store. Hopefully they'd be in the back. Maybe another employee was on duty today. He'd asked Mel and Arney to find out. If so, Rick would go in and buy them.

With clipboard in hand, he walked across the street and interviewed the manager of the print shop. The smell of smoke still hung around, but he learned they hadn't been affected by the fire. He returned to the truck where the guys were waiting.

None of the people interviewed could give any information regarding a possible arsonist. All had been gone from their stores when the fire broke out. The florist was still using one of the department fans.

Rick collected their reports and read Arney's, absorbing the information on the Hansel and Gretel shop like a sponge.

Owner of the shop was Mrs. Valerie Bernard, fifty-three, who lived in College Hill, the most affluent neighborhood in Providence. Judging by the expensive items displayed, he wasn't surprised. She was also the person Arney had talked to, because it was her signature on the bottom of the form.

The report stated there'd been no damage, but the smell of smoke still lingered. She didn't think a fan was necessary. He called out to Arney. "Did you speak to any employees besides Mrs. Bernard?"

"No. She was the only one there."

That made his mind up for him. "Give me a minute. The smoke smell is stronger on this side of the street. I want to check her place again. She might need a fan anyway."

"Okay."

He headed for the shop. When he entered, the Christmas chimes sounded. It was déjà vu. An attractive older woman with short blond hair stylishly cut who looked vaguely familiar to him was waiting on a customer, but she smiled at Rick.

He walked around, deciding the smell of smoke wasn't that bad. As soon as the customer left with a package, he approached her. "Sorry to bother you again. I'm Captain Jenner of Ladder 1. I wanted to make sure you hadn't changed your mind about wanting a fan."

She gave him a pleasant smile. "No. It's not necessary, but I have to tell you I'm mighty thankful you got that fire out in time to save the rest of us. Some of my inventory is irreplaceable. Even with the insurance, there are several dozen pyramids and signed nutcrackers that are original pieces, and priceless. They're made in Germany."

"I'm aware of that. I came in here yesterday with my daughter. She saw the gingerbread man in the window. While I'm here, I'd like to buy it for her."

The woman frowned. "A gingerbread man?"

"Yes." He described it. "It was sitting in a little rocking chair. I'd like to buy the chair, too. Maybe the items got sold. Then again, it's possible one of your employees put those items away for some reason."

"The only other person who works here is my daughter, Andrea." Blood pounded in his ears. *That's why the owner looked familiar.* He'd wondered. The more he looked at her, the more he saw the resemblance in the shape of her face and body. "She must have unpacked those items while I was gone. Give me time to check in back."

She returned in a few minutes looking at a loss. "My daughter went out of town yesterday." *With her husband or a fiancé, maybe?* Why in blazes did he care? "She'll be able to explain. I'm expecting her back this afternoon. When she comes in, I'll ask her what happened. If you call the shop after two, you'll be able to talk to her."

Rick knew exactly what had happened. She was planning to give them to Tessa for Christmas because she believed he couldn't afford it. No doubt she'd hidden them away somewhere. "I'm afraid I'll be on duty until seven. When I next have time off, I'll call around. Thank you for your help. I'm glad your shop was saved, Mrs. Bernard. It's a delightful place."

"Thank you. It's been in our family seventy-five years." She walked him to the door. "If it weren't for brave men like you, I wouldn't have had a shop to open this morning. I'm very grateful and know the neighbors around here are, too. It was a pleasure to meet you."

Now Rick knew why Andrea was so nice. *Damn.* "The pleasure's mine, Mrs. Bernard. Have a good day."

Andrea drove down the alley and parked the car next to her mom's at the rear of the shop. She was glad to be home, even if it was closer to an hour later than she'd planned. There'd been a ten-car pileup on the freeway because of black ice. No one had been injured, thank heaven, but as a result the cars were lined up several miles waiting to get around the accident scene.

She'd also stopped at her favorite bookstore and picked up a copy of a gingerbread-man book with terrific illustrations. She'd loved it as a child. Another gift from Santa.

Pressing the remote that opened the back door, she entered and could immediately smell smoke. Her heart rate picked up speed. After putting down her overnight bag, she hurried through the office to the front of the shop. Her mom saw her and smiled. She was waiting on two teens buying some hand-painted wooden ornaments.

Until they left she couldn't talk to her mom, so she went back to the office and sent

an email to Casey. She'd promised to let her
and Carol know she'd gotten home safely.
There were several emails waiting for her to
open, all of them from Gunter's family.

Andrea decided to read them later except
for one from Marie, whom she missed horri-
bly. They were close to the same age and had
a lot in common besides the fact that they'd
both adored Gunter.

Her email was inviting Andrea to meet her
and her husband, Rolfe, in the south of Spain
after Christmas and vacation until the New
Year. Would she please come? They would
pay for her flight and would be staying with
Rolfe's friend at his villa.

While Andrea stood there contemplat-
ing the generous offer and idea, she could
still smell smoke, and she lifted her head.
Where had it come from? She was dying to
know, but a steady stream of customers kept
both her and her mother busy for a couple
of hours. Finally they had a break. As soon
as the front door closed, Andrea gave her
mother a fierce hug.

"What was that all about, darling?"

"Because I love you. Because Casey and
I had a long talk, and it made me appreciate

you all over again for being the best mother in the world."

"I could say the same thing about my daughter. I'm glad you got back safely."

"Me, too. Now tell me what's happened. Why is there that smoke smell?"

"The art gallery caught fire last night around ten when everyone had gone home."

"You're kidding!"

"I wish I were. There's a possibility of arson. I was talking to Wally earlier. He said the firefighters saved as many paintings as they could, but some of the ones in storage on the third floor didn't make it. We're very blessed they got here in time to save the rest of the surrounding stores, including ours."

Andrea shuddered. "When I think of the years you've put into this shop, and then to imagine a fire threatening everything... I'm sorry I wasn't here for you."

"Don't be silly. There wasn't anything anyone could do. Life is a risk."

Yes. But she'd never thought about it until she and Gunter had been broadsided by a man who was drunk. In a flash her husband had been snuffed out. "Casey and I came to that same conclusion last night."

"Did you have a wonderful time?"

She bit her lip. "It was good to see her and Carol again, and we were able to make plans for the party on Christmas Eve, but the inn is up for sale, and Casey is very low right now. She hasn't really gotten over her broken engagement. So to answer your question honestly, I've come home a bit depressed, but it will pass."

"That settles it. After we close up tonight, you're coming home with me, and no buts."

"I'd like that," Andrea said without reservation.

"Oh—before more customers walk in, I need to ask you about a gingerbread man and a chair, neither of which I've seen. Apparently you put them in the front window display, but when the man who'd seen them before came in today to buy them, they were gone and I couldn't help him."

Andrea's heart gave a kick. "Do you remember his name?"

"He introduced himself as Captain Jenner." *Captain?* "It was his crew of firefighters along with two other crews who contained the blaze last night and put it out. This morning he came by with his men to see if I needed a fan."

Tessa's daddy was a firefighter? Here Andrea had thought he might be out of work and was too proud to accept charity. Instead while he was on duty he'd come to the shop to buy everything without Tessa knowing. Andrea didn't know whether to laugh or cry at her false assumption. The man's aloof behavior had been a disturbing mystery to her.

Her mother eyed her curiously. "Why are you so quiet?"

Just then they had another customer. "I'll tell you in a minute."

A minute turned into another hour before Andrea was able to relate the substance of what had happened, but she didn't tell her mother certain details. How could she when she didn't know what she was feeling herself? "I made a false assumption that he couldn't afford to buy the chair and the gingerbread man. His little girl was so cute and wanted it so much, I wanted to help, I guess."

Her mom nodded. "I could tell he was disappointed the items were gone. Why don't you run them to him at the fire station right now and make things right? It's only six blocks from here and will save him another trip to the shop. It'll help you feel better, too. After their heroic service, it's the least we can do for him, don't you think? But before you leave, I'd like to see that gingerbread man. Who sent it?"

"Our wholesaler in the Adirondacks. It's a sample of the new product they're introducing. I'll bring it down with the rocking chair."

Andrea went to the back room and dashed up the stairs to her bedroom. She brought down both items. While her mom was busy with another customer, Andrea placed the chair and gingerbread man next to the table with one of their three-tiered pyramids.

In a minute her mother started walking to the counter carrying a dirndl for the lady following her, but she stopped midstride when she saw it. "Oh, Andrea—without a doubt that's the most appealing craft item I've ever seen!"

"I totally agree. On the drive home from Barrow's Lake I ordered more of them and the rocking chairs."

The customer walked over and picked it up to examine it. "I'd like to buy this. My four-year-old granddaughter will go crazy over it. The rocking chair is superb, too. I think I have to have both."

"I'm sorry." Andrea spoke up. "They've already been sold, but leave us your name and number. When more come in, one of us will call you."

"Can they be here before Christmas? My friend Renee will want both for her little niece, too."

"I'll put a rush on it, but you never know."

Andrea eyed her mom before hurrying to the rear to pack up the treasures in one crate and gift wrap it. When she'd loaded it into the trunk of her car, she went back upstairs to shower and change into something fresh.

Several of her outfits had been purchased in Germany. After giving it some thought, she pulled out her cherry-red two-piece loden wool suit. She'd bought it the day Marie had gone shopping with her. Gunter had said it looked perfect on her.

Dark green braid lined the round neck and the front of the jacket. Eight ornate silver buttons the size of quarters ran down the middle to the hem at the waist. She loved this suit with its slightly flared skirt. It was reminiscent of the old-world items in the shop, but she'd worn it only once while she was still in Germany.

Chances were Captain Jenner wouldn't even be there, but she had to make the effort...because her mom had asked this favor of her. Because she realized she needed to start making an effort to get on with her life. Taking an interest in herself and caring about what she wore was a first step.

Much as she'd enjoyed seeing Casey, her overnight trip hadn't helped her spirits. It had been all talk about loss and unfulfilled lives. She'd come home actually alarmed over her depressed state of mind.

Two more hours before Rick's shift was over. While he was fueling the truck, he heard Cabrera's voice calling out, "Eighty-six! Eighty-six!" It was code that meant a woman had entered the station, but not just any woman. She had to be a total knockout. After dealing with life-and-death situations 24/7, there was nothing like hearing an "eighty-six" to set the place humming.

He watched in amusement as one by one the guys left their housekeeping duties to get a glimpse of the supposed femme fatale who'd set foot on the premises. In a minute Arney came running to the bay. He might be married with two children, but his blue eyes were all lit up and he wore a knowing grin on his face.

"There's a female here to see *you*." Rick blinked. "The guys have gone nuts. She brought a giant Christmas present all wrapped up in blue foil with a gold ribbon."

His adrenaline surged. Andrea was back from wherever. After hearing from her mother, she'd obviously come here. For some reason she'd been determined his daughter would receive the gingerbread man, even if it meant Santa came to the station in person to deliver it.

"I'd say she looks like a Christmas present herself, if you know what I mean." Rick knew exactly what he meant. Beautiful didn't adequately describe her. The expression "she looked good enough to eat" was more like it.

Arney nudged his shoulder. "You've been holding out on us big-time, boss. I'll finish the fueling while you…take care of business?"

Rick couldn't get mad at the guys for wanting him to meet another woman and start living again. No one had better friends, and they couldn't have tried harder to help him through the dark period of the past two years. They were his other family, the best of the best, but they didn't understand.

So far none of his close friends had lost a spouse. They didn't know what it was like to think of starting all over again with someone else. It took years to get to know another person, to put up with their flaws, to know their demons and still love them.

He hated being single again, coming home with no wife to hold him. He hated his empty bed, hated the loss of sharing. But he groaned at the thought of having to date again to regain that sense of completeness. As far as he was concerned, a widower was in a no-win situation.

Besides it being a new voyage of discovery that he had no interest in, it would have to involve Tessa. He had zero hope of finding another woman who would be right for him and his daughter. Would she be able to mother Tessa the way she needed it? Could he trust her with his daughter while he was out fighting fires?

It still tore him apart remembering the

nights Tessa had sobbed herself to sleep in his arms. She didn't do it quite so much now, but there were still those moments.

What if a new relationship didn't work out? Where would that leave Tessa if he had to tell her he wouldn't be seeing the new woman again? How much should he allow his daughter to get involved so she wouldn't suffer a second time? Rick had no answers, no map to help him navigate through such a treacherous sea. Better to remain single now that he was getting used to it. Be the best father he could be to Tessa.

"Thanks, old man." He let Arney do the rest of the refueling while he made his way to the front of the station. En route he was aware of the guys watching him, with the same grin as Arney on their faces.

She was in his line of vision when he rounded the corner. For the second time in two days he was knocked sideways, only this was much worse. In a word she looked so adorable in that outfit, she might be one of those hand-painted imported wooden ornaments come to life.

"You wanted to see me?"

He heard a small cry escape her lips when

she saw him. The way her chest moved beneath that fetching jacket, he had an idea she felt breathless, too. "I didn't know if you would be here. Mother told me you'd come by to purchase those gifts for your daughter. I'm so sorry she couldn't find them. I'd taken them upstairs to my apartment."

"You live above the shop?" Good grief. He swallowed hard. If that fire had spread and she'd been in there asleep…

"Yes."

"Alone?"

She nodded, answering one question for him. "I had the loft renovated after…after my last trip to Germany." Why the hesitation?

"I'm glad I found you here," she continued. "I should have realized right away you wanted to get them without her knowing about it. Since I made a promise to her, please accept this as a gift from Santa. I wrote 'To Tessa from Santa' on the box."

He reached into the pocket of his uniform for his wallet. "Let me pay you."

"No, don't! My payment was watching your little girl have one of those magical moments every child should experience. To take your money would ruin that memory for me."

Her features had hardened slightly, letting him know she meant every word.

Rick put the wallet back and moved the box behind the desk. "I'm assuming you thought I was out of work?"

"With this economy, it crossed my mind. Forgive me. I shouldn't have jumped to conclusions. I'm afraid I was putting myself in your daughter's place. I could see how much she wanted it. I was a little girl once and still know how it feels to want something more than anything." Yup. That described his Tessa. "But then Mother told me about the fire and that you and your crew had come to the shop."

"You weren't so far off the track. A firefighter's pay leaves a lot to be desired."

"Maybe so, but if it helps, just know our world couldn't get along without you. My mother sends her warmest regards."

His black brows rose. "It was her idea that you come here?"

After a slight hesitation she said, "I was glad she suggested it. We wanted to be able to pay you back for containing that fire."

Her answer deflated him despite the fact that he had no intention of getting to know her better. "I understand you went out of town."

"Yes."

"With a friend?"

"No. To see one."

That still didn't answer his question and she wasn't about to give him one. *In other words, mind your own business, Jenner.*

He'd been wrong in his assessment of her show of interest. It was evident she had no intention of getting to know him better and was simply playing Santa's helper in a way that left him humbled by her generosity. Wasn't that what he wanted? No involvement? So how come he felt more irritated than ever?

As fate would have it, he heard the gong sound. "Ladder 1. Respond to Cheshire Hotel kitchen fire on Lemon and Weybosset."

Lemon again? Her eyes widened to hear the address, too. "That fire's not far from the art-gallery fire!"

"You're right." The arsonist was on the loose again, creating mayhem, which was likely part of his intention. Another part was the euphoria a firebug felt to watch something burn that he'd set. It was a definite sickness. Rick longed to catch him and put him away.

"Duty calls. Believe me when I say Tessa and I thank you for the gifts," he called over his broad shoulder.

CHAPTER THREE

RICK WHEELED AWAY, leaving Andrea too fast for any conversation to continue, but she'd felt his sincerity and was glad of it. The man was off to save buildings and lives without a thought for himself. She admired him terribly for putting himself in harm's way.

She heard the siren and watched the fire truck pull out onto the street. His daughter could have no idea how lucky she was that her daddy was still alive to be in her life. Every time he left for a fire, there was the possibility he wouldn't come back. She knew what that was like.

Now that her mission was accomplished, there was nothing more to do but go back to work. Taking a deep breath, she left the station feeling oddly let down and walked to the parking area around the side where she'd left her car.

On the way back she passed the intersection of the hotel fire. The police had cordoned off the area. She saw three fire trucks where the men were doing their jobs with calm, methodical precision. So far she couldn't see any flames. With all their gear and helmets, it was too difficult to distinguish faces, but one of the taller firefighters could have been Captain Jenner. Much as she wanted to pull to the side and watch, she didn't dare. Maybe he'd thought she was coming on to him, that that was the reason she'd gone to the station, using his daughter as the excuse. He was so attractive she could believe other women might have tried that tactic.

But for her to show up while he was fighting a fire now would convince him she had an agenda, and he'd be justified in thinking it. Impatient with herself, she drove on and parked around the back of the shop just three blocks away.

She used the remote to go inside and found her mom was out on the floor with a young couple. They were trying to decide on the right nutcracker for his father, but were having problems. From her mother's expression, it looked as if they'd been in here a long time and she could use some help. Andrea picked up one of her favorites on the shelf and took it over to them.

"This is King Richard. If I were a man, this one would appeal to me. He has such a proud countenance and bearing."

Their response was all she could hope for and her mother rang up the sale. After they left the shop she hugged Andrea. "Oh, I'm so glad you walked in when you did."

"After taking over since yesterday, you're tired, Mom. I want you to go home now, and I'll join you after I close up."

"I won't say no to that. Are you in the mood for an omelet and salad?"

"A light dinner sounds perfect."

She eyed her curiously. "Were you able to deliver your gift?"

"Yes. The captain thanked me and wanted to pay for it, but I wouldn't let him. No sooner did he take the box than he was off to another fire. And now it's time for you to leave before you drop."

"I'm going. You look lovely, by the way. I haven't seen you in that suit for a long time."

"I think of it as my Christmas suit."

They hugged again. "I'll be waiting for you."

After she left, Andrea spent the next half hour unpacking more merchandise. Once she was through setting things out on the floor, she stood at the counter. While she waited for another customer, she read the emails from Gunter's family.

Andrea loved her mother-in-law's newsy epistles. Apparently their oldest daughter, Lisa, was expecting her third baby at the end of May.

Emily was expecting, too.

The whole world seemed to be expecting....

Though this would be as good a time as any to reply, her mind was on the hotel fire. Putting off a response until later, she turned on the radio behind the counter. The talk show station she often listened to gave local updates every twenty minutes. They were coming up on the seven-forty news. Maybe there'd be some information.

But just as it came on, she had another customer and almost fainted when she saw who it was. Captain Jenner had changed out of his uniform. Beneath his bomber jacket he wore a dark blue turtleneck and jeans. He looked amazing in and out of uniform.

In the background they could both hear the news about the three-alarm fire. She hadn't been able to get him off her mind after leaving the fire station. He and his colleagues were incredibly brave. Andrea couldn't imagine facing an inferno the way he did every time their station got the call.

"You'd never know you'd been fighting that fire they were reporting on the news."

His half smile had pretty devastating appeal. "It was put out too fast to turn into a disaster, and now I'm off duty. I'm glad to say I'll live to see another day."

She hurriedly turned off the radio. "Your family must breathe a sigh of relief every time you come home from work." How did they stand it?

"According to statistics, firefighting is only the thirteenth most dangerous job in the world."

Andrea couldn't prevent a small smile of her own, though inside she couldn't understand how he could be so glib. "Only? If you thought that would make me feel better..."

He laughed. A deep male laugh she didn't expect. One she felt warm her insides.

"Seriously, how does your wife handle it?"

"Tina didn't like it," he said without taking a breath. "The great irony is that she died of leukemia a year ago. After all the years we were married while she worried about me, her time clock was running out along with our plans to enlarge our family. We wanted to give Tessa a brother or sister, but it wasn't meant to be."

The end of dreams. Andrea knew all about that. She'd never give birth to a child of her own, and she felt as if her heart had just been squeezed by a giant hand. "I'm so sorry."

He cocked his head, continuing to stare at her. "It's life."

"I know." Her voice had an awful tremor. Time to change the subject. "How can I help you?"

"Tessa and I talked about a special gift to give my housekeeper for Christmas." Naturally he hadn't brought his daughter with him. The last thing he would want would be to get her excited all over again about the gingerbread man. "Mrs. Milne is the widow of an army officer—she came to us before my wife died."

Another widow who'd been married to a man in a dangerous career.

"Tessa loves her, so it has to be the perfect present. That's one of the reasons I've come to your shop."

"That's nice to hear. Do you think she'd like a nutcracker or a pyramid?"

"A nutcracker. Tessa was enchanted with the ones she saw in the window."

Andrea had been enchanted by his precious child. "We have a wonderful assortment of soldiers. The big ones are right over here. Maybe you'll see one that appeals to you the most."

He followed her over to the table. "They're all fabulous."

"What was her husband like?"

"She's mentioned several times he looked splendid in his uniform."

So had the man standing next to her when she'd gone to the station.

"Splendid… Hmm…" Andrea's keen eye landed on her favorite soldier, who stood fifteen inches high. She picked him up. "Meet the major general. He served in the French

Napoleonic cavalry from 1804 to 1815, the most powerful branch of the *grande armée*. Fourteen hundred officers like this one performed with great gallantry."

Their hands brushed as she handed it to him. The contact sent a warm sensation through her body. His eyes held hers for a moment before he examined the nutcracker.

"I—I love this one." Her voice faltered in reaction to his nearness. "This white uniform makes him stand out. It's an exact replica of the uniforms they wore, down to the black hat and green-and-gold trim on the cuffs and bottom of the jacket."

"It's exactly what Tessa would want to give her." His husky tone set her pulse racing. "I'll take it."

"Good. I'll find the box for it in the back and wrap it for you. Be sure to keep the box. These signed nutcrackers become a collector's item and are more valuable if you have the same box they came in."

"I didn't realize that."

She couldn't breathe until she was away from him. Good grief. She'd always heard about widow's hormones, but had never given it any thought until now. If a doctor were to examine her, he'd declare she had palsy.

After finding the box in question, she returned to the counter with it. "If you'll notice, there's a piece of parchment inside that tells you about the major."

"She'll love it."

Andrea's hands were unsteady as she wrapped the gift in green foil with a red ribbon. He gave her his credit card. She put the receipt in the sack before handing him everything.

"Mom and I appreciate your business." She flashed him a smile. "Merry Christmas. Since I'm closing up, I'll walk you to the door."

Andrea knew she was being obvious, but she wanted him to leave and never come back. It was the exact opposite of her experience with him the first time he'd come into the shop. She couldn't afford to make more of a fool of herself than she already had. He could have no idea that seeing him again had been very hard on her.

Oddly enough, she sensed he wasn't ready to go yet. If he knew she was a widow, he wouldn't be able to leave fast enough, but he hadn't asked.

A tiny nerve pulsed at the side of his hard mouth before he opened the door. "Thank you again for your generosity to my daughter. Merry Christmas." He hesitated a moment, then left.

The second his hard-muscled frame disappeared, she locked up and hurried to her bedroom to pack for her overnight with her mother. Once back downstairs, she turned off the lights, set the electronic locks and slipped out to her car.

On purpose she drove past the hotel where he'd fought the blaze earlier. Like pressing on a sore tooth that increased the pain, she needed to remember what he did for a living. There was no point in getting interested in him. After losing Gunter, she didn't want to go through another horrific loss again.

If he could be killed in a freak car accident, what chance did Rick Jenner have of surviving his world much longer? He willingly put himself in danger every time he climbed onto that truck.

To her chagrin Andrea was strongly attracted to him. His sensual appeal reached down to the deepest part of her, bringing her alive again after more than a year. She was so vulnerable right now, it was frightening. If he came near her again, intuition told her a man like him could become an addiction.

But what could be worse than getting into a relationship with a firefighter? She'd wait for him to come back to her after his shift was over, fearing that if he was late, she'd learn he'd died.

The fact that she'd turned on the radio to find out about the fire proved how anxious she was about his welfare already. He'd admitted his wife hadn't liked it. What wife could, unless she were a police officer or a firefighter herself?

Memories of the accident assailed her. *We're sorry, Mrs. Fleming. Your husband didn't make it.*

Andrea was sorry she'd met Captain Jenner, and prayed she'd never see him again. By the time she reached the house, she was convulsed in tears that made no sense. For months now she'd been trying to build a new life. Now suddenly *he'd* come along with that darling daughter of his, reminding her of what she'd lost and what she could never have. It was his fault she was falling apart.

Rick had promised to watch the Christmas special with Tessa as soon as he got home. Wishing his mind wasn't still on Andrea, he entered his house and added his gift for Sharon to the growing pile of presents beneath the tree.

Tina's parents had brought their gifts over early. Too many gifts. His own parents' presents would come later, in moderation. Tessa looked at the wrapped presents every day while she waited impatiently for Santa to come. Rick had hidden any gifts he'd bought for her in the basement along with the big present. They'd come out of hiding on Christmas morning.

He would have to work the afternoon shift that day, but the following day he had off to spend the day with Tina's parents, who lived in Providence, and then they would all be getting together. His parents and one of his married brothers who lived in nearby Cranston would drop by and then spend New Year's with him and Tessa at the house.

"Rick? Is that you?"

Sharon always said that. She had radar for ears, which was a good thing to keep them all safe. Rick thought of her as the rock who stabilized his world and Tessa's. There was no finer woman anywhere. What would he have done without her?

"I'm home. Where's the cutest little girl in the entire world?"

"I'm here, Daddy." She came running into the living room in her princess pajamas and dived into his arms, smelling sweet from her bath. He kissed her, loving this child who made his life worth living. "I've been waiting for you. Come in the family room. We're watching *Charlie Brown's Christmas.* Sharon made us popcorn."

"I can't wait!" He carried her through and sat down on the couch in front of the TV. Rick kept her on his lap while they munched and laughed. There was something touching about Charlie Brown, who'd picked out the only real tree for their Christmas play. But the dog's crazy antics as he danced on the piano brought down the house for his daughter.

"He's so funny. I wish I had a Snoopy shirt like that lady at the shop."

Rick remembered the way she'd looked in it. Tonight he'd gone back to get Sharon's gift. And to take another look at Andrea. If he hadn't given in to temptation, he might have been all right.

Who are you kidding, Jenner?

The whole time he was telling himself to stay away, he found himself entering her shop so he could feast his eyes on her in that stunning outfit she'd worn to the station. She'd produced such a sensation with the guys, he was afraid he'd never hear the end of it.

He moaned inwardly as memories of Tina passed through his mind to conflict him. But not enough to stop him from wanting to see her.

The inevitable guilt had passed. If he had to see the psychiatrist again, it would be for some other problem, because Rick had gone back to the shop when it hadn't been necessary. He'd needed to see her again and had used any excuse to drop by.

"Before I forget, Deanna called here today and has invited you to a Christmas party on Saturday night after you get off work."

"Benton mentioned it to me at the fire scene. It will all depend on my shift ending on time." He really didn't want to go. "Right now it's time for this young lady to get to bed. Let's go get your teeth brushed, then I'll read you a Mrs. Piggle Wiggle story."

Between Tina and Rick, they must have read the little stories to her a hundred times. Tina's mother had given the books to Tessa. He knew it made Tessa feel closer to her mother.

"Good night, Sharon."

"Good night, cutie."

"Thanks for everything," Rick murmured. "I couldn't do this without you."

"Sure you could." But she said it with misty eyes.

"Mom?" Andrea had just finished putting some more inventory out on the floor. "What are you doing here this morning?"

"I thought I'd get to work on the bills. Come in the back and have a bagel when you get a minute."

"I'm through now. You're a lifesaver!" The weather had turned freezing and gloomy. She was glad for the company. To her shock she'd been brooding over the firefighter who refused to leave her thoughts day or night.

Furious with herself for being this vulnerable, Andrea sat down with her mother, who'd made them coffee, too. "I'm afraid this cold front is keeping the customers away till later in the day."

"It felt like Siberia on the way over here."

She eyed her mom. "I can tell something's on your mind. What is it?"

"Your father called me late last night."

"Don't tell me Monica has left him again."

Her mother nodded.

"Didn't she do this last Christmas?"

They both chuckled. "Yes." Thank goodness her mom could laugh about it. She'd fallen out of love years ago. For a long time Andrea had prayed her mother would meet someone wonderful and worthy of her. He would have to be terrific.

"I hope you got off the phone fast."

"I did. He's driving in to Providence and wants to see you."

"Thank you for warning me, but what do you bet he doesn't?" Following her remark, they both heard the Christmas chimes.

"Maybe that's your father now."

"I don't think so. He'd call first." She got up from the desk. "I can't believe anyone ventured out in this." As she walked into the front of the store, Tessa Jenner came in accompanied by an older woman.

Andrea was delighted to see her. "Hello, Tessa."

"Hello." Her cheeks were rosy from the cold.

"What can I do for you on this wintry morning?"

A pair of green eyes looked up at her, reminding Andrea of Tessa's father. "We came to buy Daddy a Christmas present before I have to go to school. It's a secret."

"Well, how exciting!"

The older woman smiled. "I'm Mrs. Milne. I take care of Tessa."

"It's nice to meet you. I'm Andrea."

"Tessa begged me to bring her here," the older woman explained.

"I see. What kind of present are you looking for?"

Tessa pointed. "I want to buy that nutcracker over there on the shelf."

"Which one? There are five of them."

"The one with the gold crown and the cape. He has black hair and looks like Daddy."

Tessa had to have noticed him the first time

she came into the shop. Andrea reached for the sixteen-inch-tall nutcracker and brought it down. "Do you know something? You're right. He does kind of look like your daddy. This one is King Arthur. A great king. Come over to the counter. I'll get a box and wrap it for you."

"Thanks."

While Mrs. Milne handed her a credit card, those innocent eyes staring out of an angelic face looked up at Andrea. "Where's my gingerbread man? He's not in the window. Can I hold him again?"

Uh-oh. "He's not here anymore, remember?" She smiled at her.

But Tessa's lower lip started to quiver. She was about to cry. "Where is he?"

It appeared Tessa hadn't understood what Andrea meant.

Was this the real reason the little girl had asked the housekeeper to bring her to the shop? Her heart had been set on him. Andrea had to think fast as she handed the woman her package and credit card. "One of Santa's elves came for it." That was as much as she dared tell her.

She expected a smile, but Tessa's face

screwed up in pain. "No, he didn't." Her response took Andrea back. "My daddy didn't mail my letter to Santa yet. It's still home. My gingerbread man is gone! You promised Santa would bring it to me for Christmas!" She broke down in heart-wrenching tears and hugged Mrs. Milne's legs. Andrea felt as if she'd been stabbed in the heart.

"I'm sorry." Andrea mouthed the words to the other woman, feeling helpless to do anything.

The housekeeper nodded in understanding. "We'd better go." She led a desolate Tessa out the door.

After they left the shop, Andrea looked at her mother in anguish. "I didn't know what to say to her. Mr. Jenner is giving it to her for Christmas. I already made one mistake with him and didn't want to make another for fear I'd give away his surprise."

"Don't worry about it. She'll get over it when she finds it on Christmas morning. I must say she's about the cutest little girl I ever saw in my life. Except for you," she added. "No wonder you wanted her to have that gingerbread man. It was meant for a child like that."

"I agree, but she was really devastated."

"When you were her age, you had a few meltdowns, too."

"I probably did, but this seemed different. She believes I lied to her."

"Honey, you know children."

"Actually I don't, Mom. I won't ever know them, since I can't have one of my own. After this incident it's probably just as well, since it appears I'm not so great in that department."

"Andrea—"

"It's true."

Her hope for a family wasn't meant to be. She wasn't destined to be a wife and mother, and she needed to get over her self-pity. Thankfully more customers entered the store, keeping her too distracted to wallow in her deepest emotional wants for the time being.

After lunch Andrea was showing her newest customer a music box when the chimes sounded. As she glanced up and saw Tessa's striking father, she clung to the edge of the display table for support. He wore a forest-green crewneck sweater beneath his black bomber jacket. The lines bracketing his hard mouth led her to believe he was upset. It enlarged the pit in her stomach left from his distraught daughter's visit earlier in the day.

He wandered around the shop inspecting the merchandise until she was alone once more, then approached her. "I heard what happened here this morning," he said without preamble. "Sharon admitted she'd brought Tessa to the shop to get me a gift—she'd had no idea what was going to happen."

Andrea took a quick breath. "Is Tessa all right now?"

"She's fine. I had a talk with her and explained Santa already knew what she wanted without a letter."

"Did that satisfy her?"

"Enough for her to go to school this afternoon. I'm sorry she made things uncomfortable for you."

"*She* was the one who was upset. I didn't want her to think I'd lied to her."

"I appreciate you keeping my secret. Sadly, Tessa has gotten her way too often when she wants something. It's a habit I'm trying to curtail."

Andrea shook her head. "I didn't help when I took matters into my own hands the other day to grant her wish. Forgive me. It'll teach me not to do anything like that again."

His dark brows rose. "You couldn't have known the struggle I've been having, and it *is* Christmas after all, as you reminded me that first day." His comment relieved her. "Right after Tina died, I'm afraid I indulged her too much. So did both sides of the family, but my wife's in particular."

"Naturally everyone is still grieving."

"True, but I finally recognized that giving in to her at every turn wouldn't make the pain go away and was setting a negative precedent for the future."

"You sound like a very responsible parent doing the job of two on your own."

"I'm trying, but I learned quickly that I can't be the mom." *No. That job was given out to the very luckiest of women.* "My housekeeper helps with that."

Andrea smiled. "While I floundered, she handled Tessa very well at the shop."

"Sharon said she was impressed you thought of the elf idea."

"It was a stretch."

Stillness enveloped them both while he

studied her intently. "I don't see a ring on your finger, so I presume you're single."

"Yes." She fought not to show emotion. "My husband was killed in a car accident fourteen months ago. Like you and your wife, we thought we had a whole lifetime together."

More silence, then, "That's tragic." The compassion in his voice got to her.

"Yes," she said, followed by the first thing that came into her mind. "If you've come by to pay me for those gifts, your effort has been in vain."

"I already got that message at the station," he said in a grating voice. "One of my reasons for being here is to thank you properly. You've convinced me there really is a Santa Claus."

"If I could do that to a man of your age, then I'm convinced miracles really do happen."

His dark brows quirked. "A man of *my* age?"

"You're older than ten, right?" He chuckled. "What's the other reason you came in?"

He shifted his weight. "My closest friends have invited me to a Christmas get-together tomorrow night. If you're not busy after work, would you like to come with me?"

His invitation excited and dismayed her at the same time. "I'm afraid I can't, but thank you."

"You already have plans with the person who took you out of town?"

Her mother must have told him. "That's not it. I went to visit one of my best girl-friends at Barrow's Lake. She's been having a bad time lately. We're planning a Christmas Eve party for our other friend who's on her second honeymoon right now. When she gets back, they're going to renew their wedding vows. I was hoping that in making plans, it would cheer up my friend."

"Did it help?"

"I don't think so." And all the trip had done for Andrea was make her realize she was in a depression and needed to climb out of it.

"I used to water-ski there from time to time when I was in my teens. As I recall, there was an inn."

"Yes. The Gingerbread Inn. My family went there every summer for years. Casey is staying there right now. It's where we're planning the party."

"I see. You made a quick trip."

He was too observant for words. "Yes. I didn't want to leave my mother alone too long."

"She's charming."

"I'll tell her." Andrea wished he would leave.

"Is there someone else in your life, then? If so, just tell me."

His persistence surprised her. "No. I mean, there isn't anyone else."

"But you're still turning me down."

"Yes," she answered in a quiet voice.

"Is it because it's too soon for you?"

"Yes." Another monosyllable. She grabbed at the excuse, which wasn't far from the truth.

"I'm a grown man, as you reminded me earlier, so I'm going to be blunt. If I were to call you up in say a month and ask you out, do you think you would go?"

She sustained his gaze. "I'm afraid not." Andrea could be blunt, too. She had to be to protect her heart from this man whose chosen career could be cut short in a fire. She couldn't handle that kind of anguish a second time. She wouldn't.

"I have to admit it's refreshing to meet a woman who speaks her mind, even if I don't like the answer. Maybe we'll see each other again, Mrs...."

"Fleming."

If she wasn't mistaken, she saw a hint of satisfaction light up his eyes. "Even if you didn't want to know, my friends call me Rick."

After he left the shop, Andrea was so out of sorts she couldn't calm down. Once she'd closed up, she made a sandwich and watched TV to get her mind off him, but it didn't work.

After a restless night in bed she was a wreck. But by morning she refused to feel any more guilt over the way she'd let Rick Jenner know she didn't intend to go out with him in the future. His dangerous line of work loomed too negatively on the horizon for her to consider getting to know him better.

Andrea was thankful for a busy day that kept her and her mom going nonstop. But when it got to be seven o'clock, she marched her mother to the back door. "You'll be late for your party at the church if you don't leave now. I'm sure Rex Medors will be there if he's back from California." Andrea so wanted her mother to find someone to share her life.

"I hope so. Now, promise me you'll come to the house in the morning. We'll fix a big breakfast and talk."

"As long as it's not about Captain Jenner." Andrea had confided the situation to her mother, who admitted she understood Andrea's fears. Her mom had agreed that firefighting was a terribly dangerous profession, so enough said about him. "Have a good time with your group."

By ten to eight there weren't any more customers. Andrea decided to close the shop for the night, and she dimmed the lights. But before she set the electronic locks, a tall, dark figure swept through the front door. *Rick!*

Beneath his bomber jacket he was dressed in a silky black shirt and gray trousers. Her mouth went dry just watching those long powerful legs stride toward her. His chiseled male features stood out in the soft glow of the Christmas lights. He was an incredible-looking man whose male scent, combined with the soap he used in the shower, assailed her.

His veiled eyes traveled over her. "Good evening. It looks like I got here just in time. As you can see, I decided not to wait a month to see you again."

Her breath caught. "I—I wish you hadn't come."

"So do I." His deep voice resonated inside her. "I didn't like being rejected twice yesterday, so I have to ask you a question. Have you been out with another man since your husband died?"

"No. I guess it's obvious."

"I haven't been with another woman since Tina's passing either."

She wished he hadn't told her that. His admission made everything way too personal.

"To be honest, Mrs. Fleming, I don't like this attraction any more than you do. Maybe if you come to the party with me, we'll both get this out of our system and it won't seem so important."

Maybe for him... But Andrea knew herself too well. This man already did stand out in her mind. She averted her eyes, unable to think clearly with him so darkly attractive and disturbing.

"I already took Tessa over there to be with Julie, because my housekeeper needed to visit her brother tonight. Under the circumstances I don't expect to make it a late night."

"Even so, I'm not ready to go anywhere with you."

"I'll wait while you change."

"No— I meant—"

"I know what you meant. What will an hour out of your life hurt?"

More than he could possibly know. She should refuse him, but at the last moment she caved like a fool. "Will there be other children there besides your daughter and her friend?"

"Just Matt, Julie's younger brother. He's four. Why do you ask?"

"Because it's Christmastime and I feel like I should take something for the family, to be polite."

"They don't expect anything."

"Maybe not, but I couldn't go empty-handed. Give me a few minutes to pick something out." Normally when she was invited to a party, she took the hostess a gift, but in this case she'd give the children a present.

Aware of his haunting presence, she walked over to the rack on the side wall and sorted through the dirndls that would fit a six-year-old. They were all darling. Andrea picked two and then reached for a child's dark green Tyrol hat.

"You're being too generous," he commented as she wrapped each gift in different colored foil paper and ribbon.

She flashed him a quick smile. "Christmas is for children. I can't resist."

Charged with adrenaline, she hurried upstairs. After a quick shower she put on lipstick and ran a brush through her hair. She left it loose without a part. Her choice of outfit was easy. He'd already seen her in her Christmas suit and would realize she hadn't gone to any extra trouble for him. Her hair swished against the collar of her camel hair coat when she put it on.

After grabbing her purse, she went back downstairs for the gifts and set the locks. Rick cupped her elbow during the short walk to his red Toyota parked down the street.

"Busy day?"

"Yes. And you? How many fires did you have to put out today?"

"Only four."

Her body shuddered of its own volition. "Have they proved arson on the art-gallery fire?"

"Yes, but catching the culprit is something else again. The last notorious one in Providence set over 150 fires before he was caught."

"That's horrifying!"

"Agreed, but let's not talk about work tonight."

No. Let's not. What he did for a living kept her awake at night.

He made desultory conversation with her about the weather as they drove to Duncan Circle, an area not that far from downtown. The five houses on the circle were lit up for Christmas. One of the yards had a full manger display. Half a dozen cars had parked near number 42. He pulled behind another car and parked.

Rick escorted her inside the foyer and helped her off with her coat before removing his. People had congregated in the living room, which had been beautifully decorated for the holidays.

While Rick introduced her to Deanna and Benton Ames, two excited little girls came running up to him with a younger boy trailing them.

"Daddy!" Tessa hugged him.

"Hi, sweetheart."

"Come in the family room. We're watching the Grinch."

"I will in a minute. Tessa? You remember Andrea. I invited her to the party. Andrea? These are Deanna and Benton's children, Julie and Matt."

"Hello." Andrea smiled at them.

"Hi," the two children said, but Tessa gave her only a brief, cool glance.

It crushed Andrea, who was instantly aware Rick's daughter wasn't happy to see her. Hopefully she could get her to warm up. "It's so nice to meet your friends, Tessa. Are you having a wonderful time?"

The others nodded, but Tessa only stared at her. On impulse Andrea decided to give the presents out now. "I brought each of you an early gift for Christmas."

Once she'd handed them over, Julie's eyes shone like stars. "Do we have to wait till Christmas to open them?"

Andrea smiled. "No. You can do it now."

"Is it okay?" Julie looked to her parents for permission.

Benton winked. "Go ahead. I'm curious to see myself."

His children tore off the wrappings, but it took some urging from Rick before his daughter undid her gift. Julie squealed in delight as she held up her dress. Matt had already put the hat on his head.

Deanna picked up the wrapping paper. "I believe you've made our children's Christmas, Andrea. Thank you for being so thoughtful and generous."

Rick nodded. "I've been telling her she needs to be careful or she's going to give away all her shop's profits."

"Where children are concerned, it's worth it."

"Agreed," Deanna murmured. "What do you all say to Andrea?"

"Thank you, Andrea." This from Matt.

"I love my dress," Julie said.

There was nothing more than a mumble from Tessa, who held the dirndl in her hand.

"Why don't you girls go in the bedroom and put on your new dresses for us to see."

"Come on, Tessa." Julie started running and Rick's daughter followed her down the hall. Matt trailed after them.

A frown marred Rick's handsome features.

"I'm sorry about that, Andrea. I don't know what's gotten into my daughter."

Andrea could tell her appearance had been a huge shock to Tessa. To see her daddy with another woman at a party like this changed her happy child's world. That was what had caused her to dart away unable to appreciate the gift. But what she said aloud was, "I think she's still upset about the gingerbread man missing from the shop."

He rubbed the back of his neck. "I can't believe she behaved so badly."

"It's all right. Please don't worry about it."

Deanna gave them an understanding glance. "She'll get over what's wrong before long. In the meantime I have to tell you that your red suit is incredible. Where on earth did you get it?"

"In Germany."

"I thought it had to be an import. I wish they made clothes like that here. Except you have to look perfect in it the way you do."

"Thank you, Deanna."

"I couldn't agree more." Benton grinned.

"You're making her blush," Rick teased. He was wrong. Rick was the reason she was blushing, because he hadn't taken his eyes off her. "Come on, Andrea. I'll introduce you to the others."

From what she could tell, all of them were colleagues associated with the work Rick and Benton did. They talked shop, laughing and joking at the same time. One of them was a female firefighter named Susie Anderson. The attractive redheaded woman couldn't take her eyes off Rick.

Andrea understood. In her life she'd met her share of good-looking men, but few came close to Rick with his dark, almost brooding looks. Gunter's blond, blue-eyed coloring had given her husband a different kind of appeal.

While Rick was discussing the recent rash of fires in the area with Benton and the others, Andrea turned to Susie, who seemed very friendly. "How long have you been a firefighter?"

"Eight years."

Andrea couldn't imagine it. "I guess everyone asks you how you got into it."

The other woman smiled. "I come from a family of firefighters starting with my grandfather, then my father and all my brothers. I was the youngest of five children and the only girl. It's the only world I ever knew and

I became one as soon as I could qualify, to prove to my brothers I could do it, too."

Laughter escaped Andrea's lips. "You're a real heroine to me."

"In my family I had to fight for my place, and I guess it rubbed off."

"I know I'd be terrified to enter a burning building. I honestly don't know how you find the courage to do it."

"You get used to it. I'd go crazy if I had to sit at a desk all day."

"I wouldn't like that either."

"Of course, I'd give it up if the right man came along and we had children, but until that day comes…"

Sometimes the children don't come. But Andrea didn't dare tell Susie that.

"I'm sorry to hear about your husband, Andrea. I can't imagine anything worse than losing a spouse."

Her throat tightened. "It was an awful period in my life, but it's behind me now and life has to go on."

"That's so true. My grandfather died in a fire, but my grandmother was amazing about it. She's my idol."

Andrea shuddered. She couldn't handle

the conversation any longer. As if Rick had picked up on her thoughts, he walked over and supplied her with some more eggnog and hors d'oeuvres. Soon the children came into the living room once more.

A subdued Tessa walked over to her daddy looking absolutely precious in her outfit. "Aren't you coming to watch the movie?"

"Not yet."

Julie stared up at Andrea. "This is my favorite dress in the whole world!"

"You look adorable in it. So do you, Tessa. Those dresses are called dirndls. Years ago the children in Germany used to wear them all the time."

"Do you have one, too?"

"Yes. I have several. The first present my husband ever gave to me at the shop before we were married was one that looked a lot like yours."

"Is he from Germany?" Julie wanted to know.

"Yes."

"How come he didn't come to the party?"

"He died a year ago."

"Oh. So now he's in heaven." She looked crestfallen. "Do you miss him a lot?"

Andrea's heartbeat sped up. "Yes."

"My grandma died. She's in heaven, too."

Tessa's silence over her own mother's death caused Andrea's eyelids to sting. This conversation had to be terribly painful for Rick, as well.

"Your dress is really pretty. Did it come from Germany?"

"That's right, Julie."

"Are *you* from Germany?"

"No. I live here in Providence."

"She runs the Hansel and Gretel shop." Rick intervened. "They sell nutcrackers and music boxes."

"I want to see it!"

"Ask your parents to take you."

To Andrea's relief, Deanna came over to join them. It seemed as if the more Julie talked, the more Tessa clung to Rick. "You children come with me. I've got *A Charlie Brown Christmas* for you to watch."

"Daddy and I already saw it."

"Then we'll watch Rudolph. We've got a lot of fun Christmas videos."

Rick put a hand on his daughter's shoulder. "Tessa, go with Deanna."

"But—"

"No buts." He spoke firmly. "This is a party and Andrea hasn't finished talking with everyone yet."

Those green eyes glazed over with tears. "Will you come in the other room later? You promised."

"I know I did, and I will in a while."

When they were out of sight Andrea turned to Rick, sick with worry. "I think this would be the perfect time for me to leave. My father's in town and expects to see me tonight." It was the truth, but even if her father didn't make it, Rick wouldn't know that. "Will you explain to Deanna and Benton? If Tessa doesn't see me leave, it will be better. I'm sure as her father you understand what I mean."

His eyelids drooped, veiling his expression. "Of course. I'll get your coat. Deanna will watch Tessa until I get back."

"I hope your friends won't think I'm very rude for leaving."

"No. Deanna could see how Tessa was behaving and will understand better than anyone why we left. Don't you be concerned about it."

"I wouldn't hurt your daughter for anything in the world."

"You think I don't know that?" He sounded disturbed. "Until tonight I had no idea she could behave like that to you of all people. I'm sorry, Andrea."

"Please don't be. The little darling has been used to it being just the two of you. Tonight she felt her bond with you was threatened."

As a first date, it had bombed completely in ways Andrea hadn't foreseen. But it had served as a wake-up call why a relationship with Rick wouldn't work.

She saw him say something to Benton before he returned with two coats. He helped her into hers and she felt his hands tighten a little on her upper arms. It sent curling warmth through her body.

"Don't look now, but there's sprig of mistletoe above the door. All's fair," he said before pulling her close so he could press a warm, firm kiss to her lips. It caught her totally by surprise.

"Rick—" She let out a quiet gasp.

His eyes seemed to smolder in the twinkling lights. "I've been wanting to do that since we got here, and I refuse to apologize."

After he shrugged into his jacket, they left the house and walked to the car without speaking.

While her pulse still raced from that kiss, he drove quickly but expertly to her apartment, slowing down as he entered the alley. He parked outside the back entrance.

Without more words he got out of the car and came around to open her door. "Before I leave you for the night, I'm coming inside with you."

Her heart thudded. "I'm not up to company."

"This isn't in the nature of a social call. Benton has a theory about this arsonist, that this lunatic might be back to do more damage along this street, and I'm inclined to agree with him. I want to come in and check your place out thoroughly."

"You mean upstairs, too?"

"That's the part I need to see. The art-gallery fire was set on the third floor. Is your father here already?"

"Not yet, or his Blazer would be here." She felt panicky to think of him checking out her apartment. It was kind of messy, but her real concern was the fact that she'd thought she'd seen the last of him. Now he was going to invade her private space, putting them on a more intimate footing. "What about Tessa?"

"She'll sleep there tonight. Right now I want to concentrate on your shop. With all its wooden inventory, it would appeal to this pyro. You can be certain he's cased it pretty thoroughly. I know I've alarmed you, but it's better to be on the alert. It won't take me long."

Andrea pressed the remote so they could go inside. "We have the most up-to-date security system installed. The fire department did a safety check here in October."

"That's good to hear, but some arsonists have an inside track to avoid getting caught. Just so you know, the police are patrolling this area 24/7, especially after dark, so you should feel safe."

"Why do people set fires?"

He gave his shoulders an elegant shrug. "What's wrong with anyone who goes berserk in our culture? In their case they start fires to cover up a crime or pay someone back for a wrong. But I've a gut feeling this one loves to light fires for the fun of it. He wants notoriety and is the worst kind. It won't take me long to check out the ground floor, then I'll come up."

Leaving him to his work, she ran up the stairs. The shop had been so busy she hadn't had time to straighten the living room of her apartment. After hanging up her coat, she picked up some odds and ends and hurried into the kitchen to put things into the dishwasher. Once that was done, she raced to the bedroom to make her bed. He'd think she was a sloppy housekeeper.

While she was tucking the quilt beneath her pillow, he walked in. She saw his glance touch on the bed, then the eight-by-ten picture of Gunter on her bedside table. No doubt he had a similar one of his wife in his bedroom.

First he checked out her bathroom, then walked over to the bedroom window. After opening it, he looked out. When he reshut it he turned to her. "I'm glad to see the fire escape leads down from your kitchen window. A would-be intruder couldn't get in this window unless he had James Bond's scaling equipment."

"That's reassuring."

"But as an extra precaution you need dowels for all the windows upstairs and down. It'll make more trouble for him or any intruder and buy you a little time if someone wants in. What do you have for personal protection?"

"I carry pepper mace on my key chain and keep bear spray in the drawer." She indicated the bedside table.

He nodded. "Do you have a gun?"

"No. I'd rather use spray."

Without any more questions, he walked back out to her sitting room. She had no Christmas decorations upstairs. Until now she hadn't even thought about doing her own decorating, because her emotions had been in deep freeze.

But no longer. Her pulse raced just looking at him.

"You have a lovely modern apartment here. In an older building like this, it's a surprise."

"I know. Before my marriage I lived with Mom. Gunter and I were going to buy a house here, but he died too soon for us to decide on one. The loft seemed the perfect choice to remodel so I'd be close to my work."

His hands went to his hips in a purely masculine gesture. "I would have sold my house to help let go of memories if I didn't have Tessa, but any more changes to her life would have been disastrous at the time."

"They already are."

He shot her a probing glance. "What do you mean?"

"She didn't like me the other day, and likes me less after seeing me with you tonight."

Lines bracketed his mouth. "Don't read so much into everything, Andrea."

Andrea didn't want to go down this road, but tonight's experience had left her with no other choice. "Your daughter doesn't want to share you with anyone else."

He took a deep breath. "She has to share me every day when I go to work. Between all the love from her grandmothers, aunts, Sharon— from my colleagues' wives and her kinder- garten teacher, she's learning to adapt."

"That's not the same thing, and you know it. When she looked up and realized I was with you, she shut down. She feels a child's jealousy that you would give personal atten- tion to another woman besides her. *I* don't want to be that woman."

She noticed his chest rise and fall from a tumult of emotions. "This phase will pass."

"Sometimes that phase lasts years."

His eyes narrowed. "What else is going on inside you?"

Andrea tossed her head back. "Isn't Tessa's negative reaction enough to let you know this wasn't a good idea? She's so precious and you're her whole world. Your daughter needs more time."

His features hardened. "You didn't answer my question," he said, ignoring her comments. "I know for a fact you feel something for me, but you're doing your damnedest to pretend otherwise. Why?"

At his question she backed away from him. "I appreciate your checking out my apartment, but if you're through here, you ought to go back to the Ameses' house to be with your daughter. It will reassure her she hasn't lost you."

He moved closer. "I'll take your advice under consideration, but not before I get the truth from you. They say it makes you free. Do me that favor and I swear I'll never darken your doorstep again."

She wouldn't look at him. "Tonight we got this out of our system and your daughter had to pay the price. More than ever I'm not interested in a relationship."

Rick reached out and grasped her upper arms. "You're lying or you wouldn't have come to the party with me, and I can prove it." Before she could cry out, he lowered his dark head and covered her mouth unerringly with his own. There was a hunger in his kiss that ignited her desire in spite of everything she'd tried to do to stop it. Without being able to help it, her mouth opened to the seductive pressure of his.

He was right. This was what she'd been waiting for. A moan of pure pleasure escaped her throat, one she knew he heard. In the next instant he crushed her against his hard body until there was no space between them. She felt feverish as one exploratory kiss grew into another, then five, ten, twenty until she lost count. He was insatiable. So was she. It was shocking how much she wanted this ecstasy to go on and on.

"I didn't know a woman like you existed. In a matter of days you've managed to turn me inside out. Give me a chance to let me love you, Andrea."

If the buzzer outside the downstairs rear

door hadn't sounded, she had no idea how long she would have clung to him, kissing him back again and again as if he were life to her. What really terrified her was that for these moments in his arms, he *was* life to her.

CHAPTER FOUR

RICK HADN'T IMAGINED that buzzing sound. With the greatest of reluctance he allowed her to tear her mouth from his without pulling her back. "Your father?" Both of them were out of breath.

"I'm sure it is."

"This late?" It was after ten.

"Yes. He drifts in and out at will."

The buzzer went off again. Her parent sounded impatient. "You'd better answer."

"I know, but I need to freshen up for a minute."

Rick studied her features and glazed eyes. Her lips looked swollen and his five-o'clock shadow had put a rash on her face. All in all she looked slightly ravished for a first kiss, but he felt no shame. On the contrary…

"Would you like me to go down and let him in while you repair the damage?"

She blushed. "If you wouldn't mind."

"It would be my pleasure." With his body throbbing from unassuaged longings, he went back downstairs and undid the lock. He'd met her mother. Now was his chance to meet Andrea's father.

To say her graying parent in his North Face parka was shocked to see Rick standing there was an understatement. He gave him the once-over with dark blue eyes reminiscent of Andrea's. "I thought one of Andrea's friends was parked outside. Who are you?" he asked, sounding a bit territorial for the father of a grown woman.

"I'm Captain Jenner of Ladder 1 at the downtown fire station. You must be Mr. Bernard. Your daughter will be right down. Come in."

Once he was inside, Rick shut the door. Her father looked around the office. "I can smell smoke."

"That's right. There was a fire in the art gallery two shops up the street the other night, set by an arsonist. I just got off duty and came by to let your daughter know the police will be patrolling this area more heavily until January. But she needs to pay special heed when she's here alone."

"I never liked the idea of her living upstairs, but would she listen to her own father? Andrea's mother always let her be too independent, so what can you expect?"

As Rick grimaced, he heard footsteps on the stairs. "Hi, Dad. Mom said you'd be coming by."

Andrea came down in jeans and a T-shirt. Everything she wore she filled out to perfection, but that was a quick change, he thought. Rick had the strongest suspicion she didn't want her father to know anything about their evening, especially the passion they'd just shared.

She gave her dad a kiss. "You've met Captain Jenner. His crew put out that fire he was talking about. He's been making an inspection of the buildings around here and checked my fire escape to see what kind of access it has to the upstairs. He was just leaving."

Rick glanced at him. "It was nice to meet you, Mr. Bernard."

"I appreciate you keeping my little girl

safe. She shouldn't be living here on her own. Did she tell you about the bear spray?"

"Yes."

"It's good stuff. Go for the eyes."

Rick flicked his gaze to Andrea. "Be sure to get those dowels put in the windows. Good night. I'll let myself out."

After having to prematurely relinquish Andrea, whose incredible response had set him on fire, Rick had been forced to pull himself together to let her father in the door. But he'd been reeling from the taste and feel of Andrea, so that the meeting with her parent had barely scratched the surface of his mind.

However, now that he was on his way back to the party, he had time to reflect and couldn't help wondering about the relationship between her and her father. She was such a warm, demonstrative woman, but she'd controlled that emotion around him. Andrea had lived through her parents' divorce and had obviously been affected by the pain.

There was so much Rick didn't know about her, but he planned to find out. One truth was perfectly clear. When they'd heard the buzzer a few minutes ago, she hadn't been ready to let him go. Her desire was every bit as explosive as his. Both of them had experienced a moment of sheer ecstasy, and it was going to grow stronger no matter how much she might want to fight it.

But she was right about his daughter. Tessa had been jealous of his attention to Andrea. He could see that he would have to be extra careful and realized he needed to follow Andrea's advice and take Tessa home. There'd be other nights for sleepovers.

Deep in thought, he drove back to the party. Being a good friend, Deanna didn't ask any probing questions about Andrea's quick departure. He talked to everyone for a while, noticing that Susie had already left.

Rick was glad Susie had seen Andrea involved with him, in order to end any speculation or hope that he might be interested. Before he took Tessa home he sought out Benton, who was in the kitchen on the phone.

After he hung up, Benton motioned Rick over to the counter with a scowl on his face. "There's a certain pattern our fire starter has been following. One of my sources believes he's a colleague working among us. He's too good at what he does. These fires have been done by an insider."

Rick groaned. He thought of the guys assigned to Ladder 1 and couldn't imagine them going berserk. Two of them were here tonight with their wives. The thought of having to be suspicious of any of them tore him up inside. "It wouldn't be the first time one of our own turned bad."

"Nope. Watch your back, Rick. If it's true, then this guy not only likes setting fires, he's got a vendetta. I've got my guys going through every history to find out who might have it in for the department or one person in particular."

Rick let out a low whistle. "I know one firefighter who pretty well hates my guts, but I haven't worked with him for at least a year."

"Who's that?"

"Chase Hayward. When we have more time, I'll tell you about him."

Benton frowned. "That's a place to start. Let me know when you come up with any other names."

"You can count on it. Thanks for the party. Sorry Andrea had to leave so fast. Her father came into town and she had to go home."

"No problem, as long as it didn't spoil your evening."

"Not spoil. Just…complicate things a little." The result had left him breathless and wanting more of the same excitement only she could engender. "Talk to you later."

He gathered up his daughter, who'd fallen asleep on the family-room couch. She wakened enough to smile as he slipped on her parka. After he carried her out to the car and strapped her in the back car seat for the ride home she fell asleep again.

While he put her to bed, his thoughts were on Andrea. His teeth snapped together when he thought of her father showing up when he did. One taste of Andrea hadn't been nearly enough. Rick had only half believed her excuse that she'd needed to leave to get home to see him.

Trying to tamp down his charged body, he turned out the lights and shut Tessa's door. As he walked through the house, it felt like the night before Christmas. The words floated through his mind—"not a creature was stirring, not even a mouse." He couldn't believe it, but the darkness of his life seemed to have lifted and a new sense of purpose had taken over. Like it or not, Andrea Fleming was responsible for this metamorphosis.

When morning came, Tessa ran into his room to hug him. But the first words out of her mouth brought bad weather for the rest of the day. "Daddy? I wish you hadn't brought Andrea to the party."

Startled, he sat up. "Why not?" He knew the answer, but he needed to let her talk this out.

"I don't like her," she said in a tremulous voice.

"Can you tell me why?"

"Julie said she might be my new mommy and I don't want a new one." On that note she buried her face in his chest and sobbed.

Rick rocked her in his arms. What to say that would comfort this child he loved more than life itself? For the past year his heart had cried out that he didn't want another woman in his life either. But he hadn't counted on Andrea....

At this juncture he didn't dare lie to Tessa, who took everything so literally. But at the same time, he wasn't about to stop seeing Andrea. He had no idea where things were headed with her. Possibly nowhere, except that deep inside he didn't believe that.

"Right now Andrea is a friend I've met. She's been very sad."

That brought Tessa's head up. "How come?"

"A year ago she was with her husband in Germany when they were in an accident and he died."

He could hear his daughter's mind ticking over. "And now he's in heaven like Mommy?"

"Exactly."

She wiped her eyes. "I bet she cries a lot."

Rick groaned inwardly. "I'm sure she does."

Tessa touched his cheek, reminding him he needed a shave. "You used to cry."

His throat practically closed up from emotion. "We all had to cry so we'd feel better."

"Do you feel better?" she asked in all earnestness.

"Better than I did."

"Me, too."

"Then let's go eat and then we'll build a snowman in the backyard." From the window he could see snow had fallen during the night. Not a lot, but just enough to blanket everything in white. He had some shoveling to do. "I'll make us Mickey Mouse chocolate chip pancakes."

"Can I put in the chips?"

He smiled, thankful that so far they'd gotten through this tense moment in one piece. "That's your job."

Half an hour later he'd showered and shaved and they were just finishing their pancakes and bacon when he heard his cell phone ring. He checked the caller ID and saw that it was the battalion chief calling. He frowned before clicking on. "Hey, Rob—what's up?"

"Plenty. I know it's your day off, but we need all the extra help we can get. A couple of guys are out with stomach flu, one from your ladder. Just a minute ago there was a big explosion at the downtown furniture mart. We're calling in help from all over the city."

That sprawling monster? "Say no more. I'll be at the station as soon as I can." He hung up with a grimace. "Sweetheart, I hate to do this, but there's an emergency at work. Go tell Sharon I have to leave."

"Dad? Do you want more scrambled eggs?"

"No. I think I'm done, but I could use some more coffee."

Andrea poured another cup for him. He'd slept on the couch and had opened his Christmas present early because he'd be gone hunting over Christmas. She'd listened to him rant about the numskulls at his work.

While he'd turned on the TV and was grazing the channels for the news, Andrea had slipped into the bedroom to phone her mom. To her delight she found out that Rex was taking her to dinner that evening. Then the subject changed to Rick Jenner and the scene with Tessa.

"But I can't talk about that right now, Mom. I'll call you later once Dad's gone."

After she came out of her bedroom, she saw breaking news flash across the TV screen. "…case you just joined us, we're in downtown Providence on the scene of a raging nine-alarm fire that is engulfing the old furniture mart." *Nine?*

Her father whistled. "That's one mean fireball. I'd hate to be the firefighter I met last night."

Andrea was already quaking in her boots over Rick. Today was supposed to be his day off. She'd heard one of the firefighters say they could all stay up late for the party and sleep in. But word of a fire of this magnitude would reach every firefighter in the city. She hadn't known Rick long, but she knew he wouldn't stay in bed once he heard the news. Her stomach muscles tensed.

"The recent rash of fires in the downtown area seems to indicate an arsonist might be involved."

Andrea remembered what Rick had said. *I've a gut feeling this one loves to light fires for the fun of it. He wants notoriety and is the worst kind.*

When her father turned off the television, she wished he hadn't. Now that she'd seen the fire, she couldn't think about anything else. "I'd better head home to make things right with Monica."

Andrea pretended she didn't know anything about their troubled marriage. "What happened?"

"I told her when I married her I didn't want to get involved with her kids."

No. Andrea's father could hardly handle having one child of his own. What a blow it must have been to her mother when she discovered the kind of man she'd married. The difference between him and someone like

Rick Jenner, who adored his daughter and was devoted to her, was too astounding to contemplate. She found his parka and helped him put it on.

"It's good to see my little girl." After putting a new can of bear mace on the coffee table as his contribution to her Christmas, he gave her a hug. He'd always had trouble parting with his money unless it was for more ammunition or a new scope for his rifle. She thanked him and hugged him back before going downstairs with him.

"It's a fine day now that it's snowed," he exclaimed after opening the door to the alley. "But I'd rather be up in Alaska."

That was his mantra. "Drive safely."

The second he took off, she raced upstairs to grab her things, then ran down and got into her car. Once out on the street she could see the dark plumes of smoke over the downtown area, making her feel sicker as she listened to the radio report. Without conscious thought she drove to the fire station. If she saw Rick's Toyota there, then she'd know he'd been called in to help fight the blaze.

After turning into the driveway to the station parking lot, she spotted it with several other cars and broke out in perspiration. But maybe he was inside the station. She had to find out, and she went in. To her consternation she discovered there was only a skeleton crew on duty. Captain Jenner had been called to the downtown fire.

It was too late to remember that someone on duty would tell him she'd been by. So much for her avowal that she wasn't interested in any kind of a relationship with him. She wasn't, but she feared the danger of a fire of that magnitude. Her thoughts leaped to Tessa. The idea of her daddy not making it back home was too ghastly to contemplate.

She called her mother again. "Have you seen the news about the fire on TV?"

"Yes. I've been watching, and I thought immediately of Captain Jenner."

"I was fixing Dad's breakfast when he turned on the news."

"Where's your father now?"

"He's gone back home. I'll come over later, but there are some things I need to do first."

"All right, darling."

Andrea headed to the hardware store. When she came out the smoke in the sky wasn't as black as before. Part of her wanted to drive down by the fire, but another part preferred to stay in denial about him fighting the fire, so she headed for the shop.

While she listened to the news she kept busy placing the dowels and cleaning up after her father. By now the fire was 95 percent contained, but there'd been injuries. A number of firefighters had been taken to Providence general hospital. One had died on the way after a wall had collapsed on him, but no names were being given out yet.

Andrea cried out in anguish. It could be Rick, or one of his friends at the party. She couldn't breathe until she knew the truth. Without hesitation she drove to the hospital. The main streets en route had been plowed. Andrea parked underground and followed the signs to Emergency.

When she saw Rick's name on the wall chart, her heart thudded like the striking of an anvil. After inquiring at triage, she was told he was in cubicle eight and she could go back. Behind the blue curtain she found him.

To her everlasting surprise and gratitude, he was sitting on the end of the hospital bed in his uniform, breathing oxygen. As far as she could tell, nothing else was wrong with him. When he saw her walk in, his eyes suddenly gleamed a brighter green. Surrounding him were three of the foulest-smelling, grubby-looking firefighters she'd ever seen.

Arney and Jose she recognized from last night's party. "Hey, Andrea," they said in unison with a decided grin. "You're one sight for sore eyes. How did the boss find you and how come he's so lucky?"

A smile broke out on her face. "I must say you guys looked a little better last night," she teased, ignoring their questions.

"Yeah, well, now you're seeing the real us."

"Whoa—" the other firefighter exclaimed. "I know I've never seen you before." His blue eyes studied her in a way she found too bold. "Someone introduce me."

Jose smiled. "Andrea? As you can see, Chase is dying to make your acquaintance. Andrea runs the Hansel and Gretel shop downtown."

"Is that so? Well, I'm just going to have to drop by, then."

Andrea hoped he wouldn't.

"Chase swung in from another station to assist," Arney explained.

Thankfully the attending physician came

in and took Rick's vital signs, preventing her from having to make a comment. Something about the other firefighter's attitude was borderline obnoxious to her.

"Can he drive back to the station with us, Doc?"

"I can't release him for an hour. Just so you know, your captain won't be going to work tomorrow. For the time being it's home and total bed rest. Follow my advice and you shouldn't have any lasting effects."

The guys didn't sound happy about it, but Andrea rejoiced that the doctor had taken charge. For the rest of today and tomorrow he'd be safe!

After the doctor left the cubicle, Rick pulled down his mask, still staring at her. "All right, you guys. Get out of here."

Andrea thought he sounded slightly hoarse but completely like his confident self. She sent up a silent prayer of thanksgiving that Tessa's daddy had been spared to live another day.

"We're going." Arney grinned and punched him on the shoulder. One way or another the guys managed to give a physical manifestation of their affection and relief by a nudge or some other gesture.

Their camaraderie revealed they were a close-knit family of which she wasn't a part. This was Rick's element, a whole other world, and he was happy in it. She could see that. They belonged to a special club, unconsciously making her feel excluded.

Chase filed out last, not paying attention to Rick. He gave her a look that made her uncomfortable. "I'll be getting in touch with you." She wanted to call back, "Please don't."

When they were alone she urged Rick to lie back down, but he ignored her. Maybe she was wrong, but something about the other firefighter seemed to have made him tense. His next question was unrelated. "How did you know I was here?"

She told him the sequence of events, starting with her father sleeping over. Through narrowed lids he appeared to digest everything she said. "I thought you didn't want anything more to do with me."

"I don't, but the nine-alarm fire was on every channel."

"You knew it was my day off."

"True—however, it was such a huge fire I

figured you'd be called in. When I drove to the fire station and saw your car in the parking area, then I knew you'd gone on duty."

"You actually drove there to see?" A glint of satisfaction entered his eyes.

"Yes. I was concerned when I found out there were injuries…and a death."

He nodded gravely. "A father of four."

"I heard. It's so tragic." Her voice shook. "Thank heaven it wasn't you. Tessa wouldn't be able to handle it."

"I don't plan to die on her if I can help it." He bit out the words.

"I realize that."

"Now that you're here, would you be willing to wait long enough to drive me to the station for my car when I'm released?"

"I'll drive you home first," she said without hesitation. "Doctor's orders. We'll arrange for your car later. Don't talk anymore, Rick. Give your throat and lungs a rest. If you'll give me your housekeeper's phone number, I'll let her know you'll be home in another hour."

Andrea knew she shouldn't be overjoyed that he wanted her help to get home. But if he hadn't asked her, she would have worried that much more about him.

When the nurse pushed Rick outside the hospital in the wheelchair, Andrea was waiting right there in her car. The woman was tying him up in knots. He climbed inside and fastened the seat belt before they took off. If it had taken him breathing too much smoke to see her again, he wasn't complaining.

The doctor had said his heart rate was a little high. What the medic didn't know was that moments before, Andrea had walked into the cubicle. After figuring he'd never see her again unless he made it happen, he knew the shock of realizing she'd come to see him on her own had played havoc with his vital organ.

A lot could happen in twenty-four hours. He planned to use every one of them wisely.

"Are you feeling terrible?" Andrea sounded anxious.

"I'm fine."

"No, you're not."

He looked over at her lovely profile. "I'm sorry that the death of one of my colleagues alarmed you enough to bring you to the hospital. I'm sure it was a reminder of what happened to your husband. I wish you could have been spared. Tell me. What did you do with your day after your father left?"

"Besides worry about you, I bought some dowels and put them in the windows."

"I'm glad you took my advice."

"If they'll act as a deterrent, then I'm indebted to you." He noticed her hands grip the wheel a little tighter. "Was the furniture mart a set fire?"

"Benton thinks so, but it'll take a day to find the proof."

She flashed him a glance. "What's your opinion?"

"I think this particular pyro is having a field day."

"Tell me about your friend who died. How old are his children?"

"He has two teenagers and two in their twenties." Rick saw telltale tears trickle from her eyes. "Becoming a firefighter is a lot like joining the military. Everyone knows there's going to be risk."

"I'm sure they do."

He wanted to get off that subject to talk

about something more important. "Is your father going to be in town for the week?"

"No. When he comes two or three times a year, he's always just passing through."

"It's obvious you're very close to your mother."

"As opposed to my father, who was never a family man, but I'm sure you already figured that out even before you met him."

"It's his great loss for not spending time with you. He told me he doesn't like you living on your own."

"He said that because the loft is small and I don't have a guest room for him."

"Andrea? Be serious."

"I am. He hates my couch."

Rick shuddered to think what kind of father hers had been. All the lost opportunities.

Andrea pulled into his driveway, where she parked to the side to leave room for another car. He gave her a covert glance. "What are your plans for the rest of the day?"

But he didn't hear her response because he'd already opened the passenger door and Tessa had come running out of the house without boots or a parka. "Daddy—" She sounded ecstatic and flew into his arms.

After giving him a hard hug, she stared at Andrea. While his mind sought an explanation his daughter could handle, Andrea spoke up. "Hi, Tessa. Your daddy needed a ride home because he was so excited to see you. Now *I'm* going home."

His little girl shifted her gaze back to him. "Sharon said you breathed too much smoke, Daddy. I'm going to take care of you because Mommy told me to." She pulled on his hand to get him out of the car.

His daughter's sweetness made his heart quake. "You always take perfect care of me."

"See you," Andrea called to them before backing out of the driveway. Helpless to do anything else at the moment, Rick had to let her go. The last thing he saw was the sheen of her wet blue eyes before she drove off.

Tessa helped him inside the house. "Sharon says you have to take a shower and go straight to bed."

His housekeeper met him in the foyer. "We're glad you're home. I'll bring you dinner when you're ready."

Rick was so drowsy from whatever had been put into his IV, he barely made it to his bedroom. After he collapsed on the bed to get his second wind, he knew nothing more until thirst brought him out of a deep sleep. He reached for his water and drank until he'd emptied the glass.

When he opened his eyes, he discovered it was quarter after nine. That was the time he'd gone to his room last night. It meant he'd slept twelve hours! The last thing he remembered was being ordered to bed.

He rolled off the mattress, aware he was breathing more easily. He didn't feel he needed the inhaler. But once on his feet, he still felt weak. Some breakfast would make all the difference.

After a visit to the bathroom, he left for the kitchen in his sweats and T-shirt, expecting to see Sharon and Tessa, but they weren't there. He checked the note on the fridge under the magnet.

Nancy came over this morning and took Tessa home with her so you could sleep. She'll bring her back this afternoon. I'll be home from the grocery store shortly. Your friends brought your car home from the station, so don't worry about a thing.

He drank a quart of milk and munched on a banana and a couple of peanut butter sandwiches before checking his phone messages. There were half a dozen, but of course nothing from Andrea. She didn't have his cell phone number, but he *had* given her the land line number so she could call Sharon. But when he checked those messages, there still wasn't one from her.

Remembering the tears in her eyes before she'd backed down the drive, he realized she'd heard Tessa and didn't want to say or do anything to upset his daughter more. Though touched by her sensitivity, he didn't want Andrea distancing herself because of it. He'd find a middle ground for them no matter how long it took.

As he walked down the hall, he heard the sounds of the animated elf band he'd set up around the Christmas tree. He frowned. That was odd. He hadn't remembered hearing it on his way to the kitchen.

Clearly mystified, he headed for the living room and collided with a heavenly female form just coming down the hall in jeans and a melon-colored cotton sweater.

Andrea, as he lived and breathed.

A cry escaped her throat. "I thought I heard you in the kitchen."

"I needed food."

She bit her lip. "In case you weren't dressed, I didn't want to surprise you, so I turned on the elf band."

His hands shot out to steady her. Sharon must have let her in this morning. "How long have you been here?"

"Not long."

"What a welcome surprise," he murmured in a gravelly voice. Maybe he was dreaming. All he knew was that he had to taste her mouth again. He'd been hungering for it since the other night.

"No, Rick—" she begged. "This isn't why I came over." But it was too late. He'd already stifled most of the sound. In the next instant he pressed her against the wall in the hall and found himself devouring her, bite by delicious bite. What made everything more miraculous was that she was giving him breathtaking permission.

Between the flowery scent of her hair and the warmth of her luscious body, he felt transported. He forgot the time as his hands roamed over her back and hips. Being with her like this made him feel young and alive again. She clung to him in a way that told him she was experiencing ecstasy, too.

"Why do you say no when you mean yes? You're torturing me."

"It's not on purpose," she whispered against the side of his neck.

"Yes, it is. Do you have any idea how beautiful you are? How exciting?" He kissed her scented throat. "Ever since I saw you through the display window, I fought not to want you, but it happened anyway."

"I know," she admitted, sounding breathless. "I never thought I could feel this way again and I didn't want to either. I still don't." She eventually tore herself from his arms. "This couldn't be good for you. I came to find out if you were all right. How are you feeling?"

Andrea could ask him a question like that after what they'd been doing in the hallway? "Would that I could wake up every morning feeling this…marvelous." If he wasn't mistaken, she blushed. "But I need a minute to shower. Promise me you won't leave, or you'll have to put up with a grubby firefighter whose beard must be two inches long."

Her eyes studied his features. "Maybe an inch," she teased.

"By what miracle are you here?"

"I called to see how you were. Sharon said you were still sleeping and Tessa had gone out with her grandmother. When I asked if there was anything I could do, she said I could babysit while she went shopping. Since I promised to stay till she came back, you have my word I won't leave. But after your shower, you need to lie down, Rick. Doctor's orders."

He grinned. "Yes, nurse." Rick pressed a hot kiss to her mouth before disappearing, but knowing she was waiting for him, he decided it was going to be the fastest shower and shave in history.

CHAPTER FIVE

RICK MIGHT BE recovering from smoke inhalation, but the way he'd kissed her in the hallway just now, she still hadn't recovered from what she considered a more serious problem. Andrea sat down on the couch and had to acknowledge she was crazy about him.

To be alone with him for any length of time could be disastrous if she didn't want to end up in his bed. Hopefully Sharon would return soon. Rick seemed to have this power over her. When she was near him, rational thought ceased and only desire remained. Deep down she'd known from the first he could become an addiction. He already *was* her addiction. The only way to break it was to go cold turkey.

"Andrea?"

She hurried into the hallway. "Yes?"

"I'm waiting for you. It's the last door on the right."

Since she'd told him to lie down, she couldn't very well tell him it wouldn't be a good idea to join him. Her stomach got flutters when she found him clean shaven and stretched out on top of his bed in a different pair of sweats and T-shirt. He was gorgeous no matter his physical condition.

"What took you so long?" he asked in a deep voice that sent delicious chills through her body. "Come and sit by me." He patted the place next to him.

Since he didn't have a chair, Andrea chose to sit near his feet. His half smile turned her heart over. With charm like that he could get her to do whatever he wanted. "Can I bring you something to drink?"

"I'm not hungry or thirsty. What I want is to talk to you. Without Tessa, it's the perfect time to get some matters straight with us."

Andrea took a shuddering breath. "I agree, but doesn't your throat still hurt?"

"No. That long sleep did me a world of good. Finding you here has made my day."

Finding you alive yesterday made mine.

"I have a confession. On my way home

from Barrow's Cove, I bought a book for Tessa. I was going to send it to her from me, but everything has changed since then. Since I agree she needs the emotional love that gifts can't give her, I thought maybe you could slip it in with her toys from Santa. It's in my purse in the living room."

He leaned forward with a concerned expression in his eyes. "I'm sorry I came across so heavy-handed with you in the beginning, Andrea."

"But I understand why you did."

"You're an amazingly forgiving, generous person. You need to know I'm no longer going to tiptoe around Tessa where you're concerned. You shouldn't have to either, because I intend to go on seeing you. Yesterday I told her you're my friend. It gave her a lot to think about."

Andrea stood up in panic. "We can't be friends, let alone anything more. It won't work."

His handsome face darkened with lines. "Why not?"

"You *know* why."

"Because of Tessa?"

"That's a part of it."

He got to his feet. Suddenly the bedroom seemed so small. "What's the other part?"

"I meant what I said before. I don't want to get into another relationship if that's where this is headed. Just a few minutes ago you admitted you fought your initial attraction to me, too. It's because in the end I can't give you what you want any more than you can satisfy my needs. We're better off parting company for good today."

A dark brooding look descended. "How can you be so cold-blooded when just a few minutes ago we were communicating in the most elemental of ways and didn't want to stop?"

She lifted her chin. "That's called chemistry, but it doesn't supply all the other things needed to make up a relationship that will last forever."

"You and I have both learned the brutal lesson that nothing can be counted on to last forever, but a fire's been lit and it's not going to go away any time soon."

"It will if we don't see or talk to each other again," she responded emotionally.

"You think it's that easy to douse the flames licking at us? I fight fires every day.

Some become fully involved. That's what has happened to us."

Andrea shook her head. "I don't believe it can't be put out. I met that attractive female firefighter Susie at the party. Deanna told me she's single. During the time I was there, she didn't take her eyes off you. A woman with interests like yours would be a great match for you."

His mouth thinned. "What interests?"

"You both fight fires. It's who you are and what you do."

"If I'd been interested in Susie, I would have taken her to the party." His voice grated.

"Fine. All I'm saying is, there's a whole world of wonderful women out there who, given the chance, would love you and your daughter and want to start a new family with you."

"But you're not one of them."

"I can't be."

His dark expression grew forbidding. "You're keeping something from me, and I mean to find out what it is."

"Yoo-hoo, Rick."

Mrs. Milne couldn't have chosen a better moment to return. "I have to leave now." Andrea started down the hall to the living room. Rick was right behind her.

"If you want me to fix you and Andrea something to eat, just tell me," his house-keeper called from the kitchen.

"Thanks, Sharon, but we're fine right now."

Andrea hurried over to the couch to get her purse. Just as she pulled out the gift-wrapped book to give to him, Tessa came running into the house straight past Andrea. "Do you feel better now, Daddy?"

"I sure do." He lifted her in the air and kissed her. "Where's your grandmother?"

"She had to go to the dentist."

"Did you have a nice time?"

"Yes, but I wanted to stay home with you. You slept a long time," she said. Then her glance fastened on the Christmas present in Andrea's hand and she looked at her. "Did you bring that to Daddy?"

Finally a connection. Since her talk with Rick, Andrea felt she had permission to do what came next, but her heart was pounding too fast. "No. I brought it for you."

"But it's not Christmas yet."

"I thought you might like it now." She handed it to her.

"What is it?"

Rick lowered her to the floor. "Why don't you open it and find out?"

Tessa quickly tore off the paper. "Look, Daddy—it's the gingerbread man!" she cried. For the first time since the disaster at the shop, Rick's daughter looked up at her with a smile.

"I promise that Santa will bring you your gingerbread man. But while you're waiting for Christmas morning, this will be fun to read. It was one of my favorite stories growing up."

"Mine is Mrs. Piggle Wiggle."

Andrea's heart melted. "I loved those stories, too."

"My favorite's about the boy who wouldn't clean up his room."

"That's a really good one. My mother used to read them to me. I think my favorite was the Slow-Eater-Tiny-Bite-Taker Cure. But the really funny one was about the Radish Cure."

A giggle escaped. "I know. Will you read the gingerbread man to me?"

Andrea's gaze darted to Rick, whose eyes glowed with a warmth she could feel permeate her body. "I'd love to. Come and sit down on the couch by me."

Together they went through every page identifying all the characters while she read the story. Tessa was totally engrossed.

Andrea would always treasure this moment, but now it was time to go while she could leave with a good feeling. She closed the book and put it in Tessa's hands. "That was fun. Thank you for letting me read it to you. Now I have to leave."

"You do?" Andrea heard a slightly wistful tone. *Well, what do you know?* she thought.

"Yes, but I bet your daddy would love to read it to you. He's been waiting for you to come home and needs to get back to bed." Andrea's gaze flew to Rick's. "Get better soon. I'll see myself out."

To her shocked surprise, Tessa followed her to the door. "I love my book."

"I'm glad, darling. Bye." She left the house, closing the door behind her. This was the best way to end things. Cold turkey.

Before long she pulled into her mother's driveway. "Mom?" she called out when she entered the house.

"In the kitchen."

Andrea found her making the fondant for the pecan rolls she gave to her friends at Christmas. "How soon will Rex be over?"

"Not for a couple of hours. I want to hear more about you and Tessa's father."

"I left the party early to get home because of Dad. Rick insisted on doing an inspection of the shop and the loft. He said there's a fire-bug on the loose. On his suggestion I bought some dowels and put them in the windows."

"That's a good idea, honey. I'm worried about you staying there."

"I'll be fine, Mom."

"Then why are you so tense?"

"Is it that obvious?" She averted her eyes.

"I'm your mother."

"I made a huge mistake. He…kissed me and I let him."

"Was it a terrible experience?"

Andrea could hardly swallow remembering the rapture she'd felt. "No, of course not."

"But?"

"I didn't want it to happen."

"That's not really true—otherwise you would have stopped him. I'm glad this happened. Darling—Gunter's been gone fourteen months. You're free to look at another man and to care about one again. I have eyes and can see how attractive Captain Jenner is. You wouldn't be a woman if you didn't notice him."

"But there's a big problem, because he's *too* gorgeous!"

Her mother laughed out loud before she poured the hot fondant onto a buttered marble slab. "Well, you'll have to blame his genes for that. Andrea, you're so young, with a whole life ahead of you. You knew someone else had to come along one day.

"Why does the idea of getting to know this man cause you so much angst? Don't let guilt that you might be betraying Gunter's memory prevent you from getting to know him or any man better."

"It's not guilt, Mom. Trust me."

"I'm glad to hear it. So what's wrong?"

"I told you before. After losing Gunter, I don't want to care for a man whose chances of dying on the job climb astronomically because of his profession."

Her mother studied her for a long moment. "You really mean that, don't you?"

"Yes. I feel doubly sorry for Tessa. She lost her mom. One of these days she could lose him, too. That poor little girl will spend her whole life worrying about him. You should have seen her earlier. She'd been with her grandmother, but she came running into Rick's house like a rocket to hug him. It caught at my heart. Rick admitted his late wife didn't like his job either."

"Well, you have to look at it this way. He's one of those selfless men who loves what he does for a living. What would we do without his kind? In caveman days he would be the one who went out to hunt for meat to bring back for everyone," she teased. "Seriously, some men are made that way. You can only admire them."

"I do, and I've always asked myself how they can do it, but now it has hit home to me in a more personal way. Yesterday should have been his day off, yet there he was in the heart of some holocaust with no one to save him."

"I understand they work on the buddy system."

"Even so, they can die. One did yesterday."

Her mom let out a troubled sigh. "What are you going to do?"

"I have no intention of going out with him again."

By now her mom was spreading the pecans on the paper. "Did you tell him that before or after he kissed you?"

Andrea's cheeks filled with heat. "Before."

"I must say he lives up to his reputation for living dangerously. I wish I could help you with your dilemma. If you truly mean what you say and don't want to see him again, you could be missing out on a great love affair."

"Not if it's cut short." *Not when I can't give him or any man a baby.* He'd told her Tessa needed a sibling. With the right woman, Rick could have several more children.

"I'm going back to the loft. I need to clean and do a wash before work in the morning. I hope you and Rex have a great evening. I can't wait to hear about it tomorrow."

As soon as Andrea got home she lit into her housecleaning until she was ready to drop. But she still spent a restless night dreaming about Rick, and she got up early the next morning to put more merchandise out on the floor. Her mother joined her in time to wait on a steady stream of customers. The weather had warmed up, bringing in shoppers.

The chimes sounded again. She happened to glance toward the entrance and found herself staring into the blue eyes of the firefighter she'd met at the hospital. He'd warned her he'd look her up, but she really resented it when he knew she'd been at the hospital to see Rick. "Andrea Fleming. I was hoping I'd find you here. Remember me? I'm Chase Hayward, from the hospital. How's the invalid?"

He was attractive in his own way, but he had an aggressive nature she hadn't liked at the hospital, and liked less now.

"I would imagine he's still recuperating. This is my mother, Mrs. Bernard. Mom? This is one of the firefighters who came to the hospital to see Tessa's father."

"How do you do?"

His smile widened. "Now I know where Andrea gets her looks."

"Thank you. If you two will excuse me, I have some business in the back."

She wished her mom hadn't left her alone with him. "Are you looking for a special gift? We have nutcrackers and pyramids."

"No. I didn't come to buy anything. I wanted

to ask you out to dinner this evening, unless you and the captain are an item."

This man would be the last person she'd ever want to go out with, but how to do this tactfully so as not to offend him or affect his relationship with Rick? "I'm friends with the captain's daughter and haven't been out with another man since my husband passed away. I still miss him terribly." Though it was the truth, she'd gotten past the pain since meeting Rick.

"I'm sorry you lost your husband."

Andrea had nothing more to say to him. "So am I. If you'll excuse me, I have more customers waiting."

"Andrea?" Her mother walked up to her with a serious expression. "You're wanted on the phone. I'll take over for you." Andrea had the impression it was Rick, and she went to the back of the shop. Unfortunately she was breathless when she picked up. "Hello?"

"I'm sorry if I'm getting you at a bad time, but this couldn't wait."

"What's wrong?"

"Yesterday you walked out on me and Tessa. After you left, she told me she wished you had stayed to read some more books to her. There's been a breakthrough."

"That makes me happy. She's very precious," Andrea said in a shaky voice, "but I'm afraid I can't talk any longer." Thrilling as those words were, it didn't change her decision.

"Don't hang up. Your mother just told me Chase Hayward was in the shop."

She blinked. "Yes?"

"Is he still there?"

"I don't know."

"What did he want?"

There was no use lying to Rick, who sounded so terse. "He said he didn't come to buy anything—he wanted to invite me out to dinner."

"What did you tell him?" His voice sounded an octave lower.

"That I'm still mourning my husband. Then Mom told me I was wanted on the phone. What's wrong?"

"Do me a favor and drive over to my house as soon as you can get here. Ask your mom if she'll take over while you're gone. This is important, Andrea."

"Rick—"

"Just do it!" He sounded fierce before she heard the click and the dial tone.

Stunned by the call, Andrea found her mother on the shop floor and told her Rick needed to see her right away. "It sounded like an emergency."

"Then go, and don't worry about me."

Andrea grabbed her purse and coat before flying out the back door. She couldn't imagine what was going on, but knew it had to do with the other firefighter. During the drive she reflected on the scene at the hospital and Chase's cocky behavior. Andrea felt as if he couldn't have cared less about Rick's condition. He hadn't acted the same as Rick's other friends and colleagues.

To her surprise Rick came outside when he saw her drive up. His long, well-honed body was clothed in jeans and a polo shirt, drawing her gaze. Andrea parked behind his car. He walked over to help her out. "Thank you for getting here so fast."

"It sounded urgent."

"I know I frightened the hell out of you, but I had to do something to get your attention." He cupped her elbow as they walked into the house.

"Where's Tessa?"

"Sharon's gone to pick up her and Julie at school. Let's go in the kitchen where we can talk."

"You sound much better today."

"I'm fully recovered." In the next breath he pulled her into his arms and gave her a long, hungry kiss. To her shame it went on and on and left her gasping for breath once he relinquished her mouth. "I had to do that before we talk about Chase Hayward."

She saw his lips tighten. So she hadn't imagined tension between them at the hospital. "I hope you know I'm not interested in him." Andrea decided to tell him everything. "I'm sorry to say I didn't like him. Among other things he has an attitude problem."

"There's a lot more wrong with him than you can imagine." At this point the glaze of desire in Rick's eyes had vanished, to be replaced by the dangerous glittering look he'd given her in the shop that first morning. He let go of her arms so she could sit down at the table.

"I take it you're not friends."

"Anything but." His hands went to his hips in a totally masculine gesture. "We joined the department at the same time eight years ago and worked at the same station for three years. He always saw everything as a competition. After his divorce, he got worse. When I was promoted to captain of my own ladder truck and transferred to the station I'm in now, it was a great relief.

"A year later I learned he'd made captain at our original station. On the rare occasion when we were fighting the same fire, he was openly hostile to me when the other guys couldn't hear him. Arney confided that Chase was jealous of me because not only had I been promoted earlier than him, but I'd made captain of the ladder truck in the downtown station."

"Why would he care?"

"Because our station fights the most dangerous fires. It's a matter of pride with him."

With those words it felt as if a bomb had exploded inside her. Rick had just given her more reason to walk away from him as soon as Sharon got back.

"That had to have been a wound to his colossal ego," she murmured.

"You could say that. He was the only firefighter I knew who didn't come to my wife's funeral. As Benton said, he was conspicuous by his absence."

In a fraternity like theirs, Andrea realized any absence would be noticed. "Then I don't understand why he came to the hospital with the other guys to see you."

"I've been asking myself the same thing, but I think I know now." His hands gripped the back of one of the chairs. "How long was he there at the shop?"

"I don't know. I left first."

"Let's call your mother and find out. Ask if he ever went into the back area. Put it on speakerphone."

Rick had a definite reason for asking that question. Andrea was positive it had nothing to do with her. She reached into her purse for the phone and made the call. When her mom answered, she asked about the firefighter who'd been in the store earlier. Andrea explained this call was at Rick's request.

"Well, he wandered around the shop for about five minutes looking at all the merchandise while I waited on some other customers. He eventually picked out a smoker and paid for it. Then he thanked me and left."

"Rick wants to know if he went in the back."

"No."

"Thanks, Mom. I'll explain later."

She clicked off and looked up at Rick, who'd started pacing. "Tell me what you're thinking." His grim expression made her nervous. "Obviously something is very wrong."

He came to a standstill. "Didn't Hayward tell you he wasn't there to buy anything?"

"Yes."

"But in the end, he bought something from your mother." Lines marred his handsome features. "I don't want him harassing you again."

"After what I told him, I'm sure he won't."

Rick averted his eyes. "Excuse me for a minute while I make a phone call. Don't move." He gave her a long, hungry kiss that left her thoroughly shaken and trembling before he let her go and walked out of the kitchen.

While she sat there dazed, Tessa came running into the kitchen from the door leading into the garage. She was carrying a packet and Sharon was right behind her. "Hi, Andrea!"

What a change in her! Andrea thought. "Hi yourself!"

"Where's Daddy?"

"He's on the phone in the other room."

"Is he still in bed?"

"No."

"That's good. I want him to get well really fast."

"So do I. How was class today?"

"Rodney Carr threw up by the teacher's desk. He ate corn dogs for lunch. Everybody ran out in the hall."

"Oh, dear."

"His mom had to come and get him. Mrs. Riley said the flu is going around. If we start to feel sick to our stomachs, she doesn't want us to come to class."

Amazed at all the information pouring out of her, Andrea tried to stifle her laughter. Wait till she told Rick. "Did you like the corn dogs?"

"No. They're yucky."

"Then I bet you're hungry," Mrs. Milne interjected.

"Yes. What are we going to have for dinner?"

"I thought I'd make tacos."

"Um. Daddy and I love those. He's always hungry and eats anything."

That child had worked her way into Andrea's heart. "Well, that's lucky. Somewhere I read that a firefighter consumes a lot of calories when he's on duty." She was still trying to stifle her laughter.

Sharon rolled her eyes. "That makes it easy for me. My husband was a picky eater."

"So's my father," Andrea admitted.

"Tessa? Go find your daddy and wash your hands while I fix you some apple dippers."

"Okay. I'll be right back."

A few seconds later she could hear voices in the hallway. When Rick's deep, male belly laugh resounded in the air she knew Tessa had told him about what had happened at school. After his dark mood, the happy sound was a revelation.

CHAPTER SIX

RICK WALKED TESSA back to the kitchen and beckoned to Andrea from the doorway. "Sharon? Benton just arrived. The three of us will be in the den until dinner."

She nodded. "Tessa's going to help me grate the cheese."

"Hurry, Daddy."

"We won't be long," he promised.

When they reached the hallway, Rick pressed a swift kiss to Andrea's unsuspecting lips. "I'm in agony waiting to be alone with you, but Benton wants to talk to you first."

She blinked. "Why?"

"I'd rather he told you. While you were driving over here, I phoned him and told him about Chase. He said he'd be right over."

When they walked into the den, Benton greeted Andrea and told her to sit down. Rick sat in the chair next to her. "I'm glad you came so quickly. As Rick has indicated to you before today, someone has deliberately been setting fires in the downtown area. We suspect Chase Hayward is responsible."

A gasp escaped her throat. Her anxious eyes searched Rick's. "You think our shop is next?"

"Since he saw you in my hospital room and found out it's your shop, I'm positive."

Benton nodded. "I've been on the phone with your mother. At this point she's very concerned, especially for you."

"That shop has been in the family for years. I had no idea you'd been talking to her."

Benton cocked his head. "It pleased Hayward to find out Rick had been injured in the fire. That's why he came to the E.R. He needed to inspect the damage. That's what arsonists do. But he failed to snuff him out, so he's unlikely to quit."

Andrea lost color. "That's so sick."

"You're right. When he set the art-gallery fire, he would have cased the outside of the buildings, front and back, on the street. This afternoon he cased the downstairs of your shop. By now he's done his research and has probably found out that you live upstairs. He's probably come by Rick's house and seen your car in the driveway."

Rick felt her shudder, even though they weren't touching.

"Since he visited your shop this afternoon, we're fairly certain he would enjoy it if you got hurt—or worse—in the fire he plans to set. It would be his ultimate revenge against Rick."

Her head jerked in Rick's direction. "That's horrifying. How have you stood working around someone that mental?"

Rick reached out to give her arm a reassuring squeeze. "As I told you earlier, we don't bump into each other that often. But the point is, nothing's going to happen to you or your mother. I swear it."

"I know that."

Benton said, "We've set up a sting operation using help from the parcel service that delivers freight to you. If Hayward doesn't start a fire tonight, then we'll have a trap set for tomorrow night or any night in the near future. With your cooperation, we'll catch him."

"We want to help!" she assured him. "I can't bear for that man to destroy more businesses and lives."

"Amen," Rick muttered.

"Naturally we hope he'll show up tonight. Of course you won't be there. But if he decides to wait until another night, here's the plan. In the morning we want you and your mother to drive to work together. While she's out on the floor, we'd like you to answer the buzzer. One of my men will come to your back door disguised as a parcel service employee. He'll bring in the freight.

"Once inside, he'll take off his uniform and you'll put it on. He'll be wearing a wool hat. It's the key. Make sure none of your hair is showing. While your mom shows him upstairs, you'll hurry out to the truck and the driver will take you to an undisclosed location, where one of our men will drive you to your mother's house. We already have police surveillance on your mother's home 24/7 to keep both of you safe."

Rick could feel her trembling. Just when he felt he'd been making real progress with her and Tessa, Hayward had chosen this moment to get his revenge. Rick hated it that because of his association with Andrea, she and her shop were being targeted by that maniac.

"Tomorrow your mother will work until she decides to close," Benton explained, "then drive home to be with you. One of my men will hide in your apartment for as long as it takes to capture Hayward. In the meantime you'll stay at your mother's and the two of you will continue doing business as usual. Do you think you can handle this?"

Andrea nodded.

"Good." He got up from the table. "Sorry this is such an ugly business, but it should be over soon."

"Stay in here, Andrea," Rick whispered before he walked Benton to the front door. The second he left, Rick returned to the den and found her with her head buried in her hands.

He knelt and covered her hands with his own. "*Andrea*...I know this terrifies you."

Slowly she lifted a tearstained face. "I have to admit I don't like the idea of Mom being involved. If anything happened to her, I don't know what I'd do."

Rick kissed her wet cheeks. "I promise that

neither you nor your mother will get hurt. I swear it."

"I believe in you." Her voice trembled. "That's part of what's wrong. Chase is after you. It's horrible and so strange because it's one nightmare I hadn't thought of."

"What do you mean?"

Andrea wiped her eyes and sat all the way up. In the soft light of the room her hair fell in waves around her shoulders like spun gold. The contrast with her brilliant blue eyes set in an oval face was stunning. His gaze traveled to the passionate curve of her mouth. He could never get enough of it, not in a lifetime.

"I don't know where to start."

He shook his head. "You puzzle me, Andrea. I never know where I am with you. How about a little honesty over what is really going on with you? I take it you were very much in love with your husband."

"Yes."

"So was I with my wife. Meeting you has come as a shock. I'm feeling and thinking things I never expected to experience again. I can see it's the same for you."

"You know it is." She half moaned the

words. "It seems way too soon to experience emotions this strong."

"Is guilt the reason you keep pulling away?"

"No," she answered truthfully. "Like you, I'm overwhelmed with feelings I thought had died with Gunter. But you have a child and I don't want to hurt her. She's too important."

"Why would you hurt her?"

"If I see you any more, then she'll grow more attached. I mustn't let that happen."

"In other words, you intend to carry out your plan to stop seeing me."

"I can't go on like this."

He breathed in sharply, because she sounded as if she meant it. "In the name of heaven, why not?"

"Because…you're a firefighter."

Rick shot to his feet. "*That's* the real reason?"

She reared her head, causing her golden hair to swish against her cheeks. "It's the most important one."

"So there are other reasons, too?"

"Let's just say that your line of work trumps everything else. I couldn't stand to get into a relationship with a man who puts himself in harm's way every time the truck leaves the station. I'm not made of the same stuff as your late wife. I'm a coward."

"That's an excuse for what you're not telling me."

Her eyes searched his. "Why don't you humor me and tell me why you became a firefighter. What is it about the job that sends you into a raging fire time after time? Are you going to tell me you come from a long line of firefighters?"

Interesting it had taken this long before she asked. "Nothing of the sort. One grandfather was a college professor, the other worked for a newspaper. My father is a chemical engineer who heads projects for a gold refining company in Cranston, where I grew up. My elder brother is a dentist.

"Though I started out in engineering in college, I'm afraid my heart wasn't in it. During my last year I dropped out and became a firefighter. I knew it would be a disappointment to my family, so I never talked about it. But from the time I was ten, I always wanted to be one."

He'd finally captured her attention. "What happened when you were ten?"

"I was at a neighbor's house, upstairs with

my friend Denny. It was a summer afternoon. We were playing with my dog, Shep, and teaching him tricks. His mom was downstairs cooking dinner. I learned later that the deep fat fryer caught on fire and it set the whole kitchen ablaze. We didn't know anything was wrong until we were both enveloped in suffocating black smoke and couldn't see our way to the stairs."

Andrea covered her mouth in horror.

"We opened the windows to get out, but there was nowhere to climb down. I heard the fire engines coming and screamed to them for help, but the smoke was so thick I knew I was going to die. I couldn't see or hear Denny or my dog. All I remember after that was someone grabbing me and carrying me down a ladder to the ground."

"Thank heaven—" In the next breath Andrea threw her arms around him, almost strongly enough to knock the wind out of him.

"I told him my friend and my dog were still up there. In a minute both were brought down unconscious, but one of the firefighters put oxygen masks on Denny and Shep and saved them. Denny's mom was hysterical until she realized we'd made it out alive.

"Later in the week our two families went to the fire station to thank the two firefighters who saved our lives. Denny and I decided they were gods and we wanted to be just like them."

"I can understand that." Her voice shook. "Did he become a firefighter, too?"

He hugged her tighter. "No. He went into the military and has made it his career."

"One way or the other, you're both saving people, but I can't imagine going through such a horrendous ordeal."

"It was awful. I had nightmares about it for years until I started fighting fires and helping people trapped in an inferno. Now I don't have those bad dreams anymore."

"I'm so glad of that." Andrea sobbed quietly. "Forgive me for getting upset over your work. I haven't meant to judge you. What you do is so heroic. You save lives every day. You saved a lot of the art gallery and prevented our shop from burning. There are no words to tell you what I really think of you."

"If that's the case, I'll ask you this again. Do you wish we hadn't met?"

"Yes."

"Surely you can't mean that."

"But I do. I may feel a strong attraction to you, but it doesn't follow that I could handle a permanent relationship. As you can see, I can't." He heard the tremor in her voice. "In just a week's time you've been in the hospital with a problem that could have injured you forever, and it's Chase's fault. Someone died in that fire, a man with a family.

"I can't stand it that there's a guy out there from your own profession trying to kill you. Even if he's caught, you'll be out fighting fires again and could perish like your colleague. I don't want to be around when that happens, because one day *it will*."

Rick ground his teeth. "Did you ever get professional help after Gunter died?"

She stirred restlessly and pulled away. "No."

He studied her features. "Have you considered that this fear of yours stems from his sudden death?"

Andrea had to be disturbed by his questions, because she moistened her lips nervously. "I'm sure his death plays a part in my fear, but it goes much deeper than that."

"Then explain it to me. Help me to understand."

She hugged her arms to her waist. "You don't want to hear it."

"Let me be the judge of that. We're talking about our lives here. Our happiness. I've just met this incredible woman and already you're distancing yourself from me. Help me understand."

He had to wait a minute for an answer.

"My first recollections of life were of a loving mother and an absentee father. He lived to go hunting. If he wasn't at work, he was out at the shooting range with his best friend Frank, who was also a hunter. I hardly saw him from season to season and hated it every time he walked out the door with his rifle.

"Frank was married, and he abandoned his family to hunt, too. I knew people got killed hunting and begged my dad not to go. He'd just pat my head and tell me to be a nice girl for Mommy. After he'd leave, I'd run to my room and pray and pray he wouldn't die."

"Andrea—" Rick was devastated.

"One day my fears came true. He and Frank got shot by accident. Frank died and

Dad was hospitalized for a gunshot wound in the arm. While he was recovering, that was the longest time he ever spent at home. But it wasn't a happy time for me or Mom, because that's when he started drinking."

Rick grimaced, imagining her pain.

"He cried for his friend all the time. It felt like he loved Frank more than he loved me and Mom. When he got better, he didn't stop hunting. He went again and again with hunting friends. Every time he walked out the front door, my heart died a little more, but I knew my pleas would never stop him.

"By my teens I realized he didn't love us like he loved hunting. He provided for us, but with insight I saw that he was so selfish, he always put us last. Mom did the only thing that made sense and divorced him. She'd always had the shop to run, and that was her solace. We had peace after he left.

"The only reason I had a visit from him the other night was because he needed a place to stay and didn't want to pay money to go to a hotel. His third wife doesn't like his hunting either.

"You know what he left me for a Christmas present? Another can of bear mace."

What Rick was listening to made him ill.

"When I met Gunter and fell in love, I was so glad he didn't hunt or do any dangerous sports. I knew my marriage would be ideal because he'd always be there and always come home to me and the family we planned to have. But he died, too," she said in a pained voice that ripped up Rick's insides.

On a groan he reached for her. After wrapping his arms around her, he rocked her for a long time, never wanting to let her go. But slowly she eased away from him and wiped her eyes.

"I've had enough of death and the pain of worrying. Meeting you has proven to me there are other men out there who can attract me. Perhaps one will become special, but he won't do any of those thirteen most dangerous jobs you talked about, maybe not even the first thirty.

"When I see how well Tessa handles your work, I marvel. Maybe being born into a firefighter's family makes all the difference. More important, she knows she comes first in your heart and is loved beyond everything. She's very lucky. I'm quite crazy about her. That makes this extra hard, because she's at the age where she wants and needs a mommy, but I can't allow her to become attached to me.

"So, as much as I'd like to lie in your arms and feel alive again, I know of the terrible price that will have to be paid the first time I learn you're off to another fire. I simply wouldn't be able to handle it."

He shook her gently. "There has to be a way for us to work this out, Andrea." Rick couldn't conceive of not being with her. After hearing about her father, all he wanted to do was love her.

She shook her head. "You know there isn't. Admit that having felt the sparks with me, you'll meet another woman out there who makes you happy again. She'll love you without fear of how you make your living and she'll love your daughter. Best of all, she'll give you more children."

Rick moaned, trying like the devil to process everything she was telling him, but something still wasn't connecting.

"I happen to know she'll consider it a privilege to be loved by you. You're a remarkable man, Captain Jenner. Fearless. Honorable."

"Don't set me up to be something I'm not."

She laughed sadly. "Tell that to the birds. I'm going to try to forget you, but it may not be possible. Nevertheless I intend to go my own way once Chase Hayward is caught in the act. Now I'm going to slip out your front door and meet Mother at the house. You need to eat and sleep. Tell Tessa my mommy needs me and I had to leave. She'll understand that."

Andrea kissed his jaw and left the den. He followed her to the front door and watched her drive away. Rick could have gone after her, but knew this wasn't the right moment. There was a fight going on inside her. He needed to give her more time, but one thing was certain. No way was he going to let her walk out of his life.

Hours later he put Tessa to bed, then lay down on his own waiting for Benton to phone and tell him that the Hansel and Gretel shop had a nocturnal visitor. But the call never came. It meant Chase had something else in mind. For the rest of the night Rick wrestled with his thoughts, wondering what his next move might be.

The man had hated Rick for years. For him to go to the shop and ask Andrea on a date was a premeditated move on his part to bait Rick. The lowlife had probably been stalking her every move.

Rick's gut told him Chase meant to harm her. Maybe he didn't plan to set the shop on fire, but this night would have given him the perfect opportunity. He'd been in the cubicle of the E.R. when the doctor had told Rick he wouldn't be able to go back to work for a couple of days.

Armed with that knowledge, Chase probably had something much more evil in mind while he assumed Rick was still out of commission. The fear of what he might be planning brought him to his feet in a cold sweat.

He checked his watch. Five-thirty a.m. Without hesitation he phoned Benton with his newest suspicions. After they made a plan, he hung up and got dressed, opting for his hiking boots and parka. He left Sharon the message that he'd had to leave early for work.

One way or another he was going to beat Chase at his own game. It was only a matter of time…. He'd promised Andrea he would protect her and her mother. He wouldn't be able to breathe until Chase had been caught and put away.

Instinct prompted him to drive over to Mrs. Bernard's home, but he parked alongside a group of cars three blocks away at an all-night shopping center. The streets were dry. Armed with his licensed concealed weapon and binoculars, he stole through a series of people's backyards, some with snow, others where the snow had melted.

He climbed a leafless tree in order to keep watch without being detected. Someone intentionally looking for him might see him, but that was a chance he had to take. Rick braced himself against a sturdy limb and ate a couple of granola bars while he waited.

After a nearly sleepless night, Andrea and her mom left the house at nine in her mom's car. Andrea left hers in the garage. Since she would be putting on a parcel service uniform later, she'd dressed in jeans and a sweater she could wear under it without problem.

She knew that if Chase Hayward had tried to get into the shop last night, Rick would have notified her by now. She was thankful he hadn't yet tried to burn their business down.

En route they stopped for bagels and coffee before they let themselves in the back door. Over breakfast Andrea eyed her mother through tears. "If anything happened to you…" She couldn't finish the thought. "You're the bravest person I know, Mom. I'm practically falling apart over this situation, but you remain fearless. How do you do it?"

"I'm as nervous as you are deep down."

"To think that firefighter would hate Rick enough to want him dead." Her voice shook. "I can't bear it."

"Chase's jealousy of Rick is a terrible thing now that it's out of control. But the police and the fire department are all working on this case. I have faith he'll be caught. Don't you?"

Andrea couldn't swallow the rest of her bagel. "Yes, but it's all so hideous. Rick risks his life every day, and now he has to worry that someone's after him with a vengeance. Now it's put him and the shop in danger, including my mother."

"We're being protected, honey, but none of us is exempt from the ugliness of this world."

"I know, but this must be so awful for him. I don't know how he goes on." She jumped up from her chair. "What if he dies?"

Her mother stood and put an arm around

her. "I have a feeling you're remembering that agonizing time when you were in the accident. Such deep-seated pain can color your emotions for a long time. Just remember you're not in that situation now and Rick is very much alive. Hold on to that thought."

"I'm trying." She sniffed. "Tell me about Rex."

"We're going to dinner and the ballet tonight."

"I know. I guess what I'm asking is, how do you feel about him?"

Her mom smiled at her. "I like him a lot. We're going out tomorrow night, too."

"*And* Saturday night?"

"Yes."

"I'm so pleased for you, Mom," Andrea said with a slight glistening in her eyes.

"Oh, darling, it will happen for you, too," replied her mom.

Minute by minute the neighborhood came to life—people leaving for work, other people out walking their dogs, kids headed to school. By eight-thirty he noticed more traffic. Several vans for satellite TV, a moving van.

His pulse raced the moment he saw Andrea and her mother leave the house by the front door. The binoculars hanging around his neck gave him a close-up of the woman who'd turned his life upside down over the past week. This morning she'd dressed in a parka over her jeans. Her gilt hair gleamed in the sun.

Andrea's mother backed them out of the driveway and they drove down the street. Once they were gone, he figured Chase would come now if he was going to. But if Rick was wrong, then he'd revert to plan B and start stalking him.

When ten more minutes had passed, Rick decided he'd made a miscalculation. After tucking the binoculars inside his parka he was getting ready to descend when he saw a work truck pull up in the driveway. His adrenaline kicked in and he pulled out his field glasses. "Bailey's Garage Door Service."

A man in a work uniform and a blue cap got out with a satchel, but Rick recognized his height and build immediately. *I've got you, Hayward.* His profile met the criteria of the sociopath, particularly in the areas of no remorse and illusions of grandeur.

While he got busy opening the garage door, Rick made his descent. When he'd disappeared inside, Rick sprinted across the yard and over a fence. With stealth he approached the small window on the side of the garage.

Chase was hunkered down by the driver's side of the car. Sure enough, he was planting an explosive device that would kill the person who opened the car door. He'd left the garage door open so he could get out fast and then close it before driving off.

Rick stole to the opening, then crept up behind him. Close enough now, he put an arm around his neck and squeezed until Chase was forced to let go of the device. The next thing Rick knew it detonated in a burst of flame. At that point the garage filled with police and he was hauled into an ambulance, where the paramedics got to work checking him out.

Benton climbed inside and rode to the hospital with him. "Hey, buddy. Nice work. You've caught our firebug, who took the hit with his own bomb. Thank goodness you got off light. Just some hair was singed."

"What about Chase?"

"I'd say he was burned over a third of his body, including his hands. If he'd been farther inside the car, there'd be nothing left of him."

Thank goodness. He'd never be able to hurt Andrea again.

Andrea and her mother both heard the Christmas chimes at the same time, cutting off further conversation.

"I'll go wait on our customer while you watch for the truck. It should be here any minute. Are you still nervous?"

"I'm more angry than anything else right now. I want Chase in jail."

Andrea felt a moment of shock when she realized the man coming into the shop was Benton. Alarm bells went off in her head and her heart began to race. Something must have gone wrong, and Andrea found she could barely draw breath.

"What's happened? Is Rick all right?"

"He's fine. Our arsonist made his near fatal move."

Andrea gasped. "Where? You mean he's been caught?"

"Caught and in the hospital under guard. He broke in to your mother's garage after the two of you left for work this morning. He was planting a bomb in your car when Rick surprised him. In the struggle, it detonated too soon and Chase received burns over a third of his body."

Her mind reeled. For a minute she couldn't breathe. "But Rick was supposed to be home resting under doctor's orders!" she cried. "How could he be at my mom's?"

"I'll let him explain after he's released from the hospital."

"He's in the hospital, too?" she cried in absolute panic.

"Not in the way you're imagining. He's only there to be checked out and give our team information."

Tears had pooled in her eyes. "How bad is he, Benton? I want the truth!"

"A little singed hair and eyelashes. He's fine, Andrea. I promise you."

She groaned aloud. "He's still supposed to be in bed recovering from smoke inhalation!"

"Let's be thankful he followed his instincts and figured out what Chase had in mind before it was too late. Rick is never wrong. He'll receive another citation for this."

"I'm not surprised, but it doesn't take away from the fact that he could have died!"

"But he didn't—you can't think that way, Andrea. Between you and me I'm thankful things turned out as they did. Otherwise I shudder to imagine what would have happened to you the next time you got in your car."

Rick... He'd put himself in jeopardy to save her life. It was too much.

"Our city of Providence is safe from who knows how many fires he would have set off until he was caught."

"C-can I go visit him?" Her teeth had started to chatter.

"Rick's at an undisclosed hospital with police officials while they wind up this arson case. He'll phone you later. You and your mother can go home at any time, but the garage is still a crime scene. Your mother will have to park out in front.

"When all the damages are assessed, we'll let you know how soon your car can be restored to you. I'm sure your insurance company will give you a loaner car."

"Thank you for telling me that," she said, but her mind was on someone else. "What about Tessa?"

"She doesn't have any idea what's gone on. My wife will be driving her and Julie to school and picking her up at the end of the day. Stop worrying."

Benton could say that because he was a man who, according to Rick, had been a firefighter first. Men thought differently than women, especially these heroic men. "I wish I could."

He put a hand on her shoulder. "The menace is over, and I happen to know Rick's fine, because I've seen him and I've been on the phone with him."

"You have?"

"I wouldn't lie to you. He'll get in touch with you when he can. We're all breathing a sigh of relief that you and your shop are safe."

"You're very kind, Benton. I appreciate everything you've done to keep us safe." She looked over to her mother.

"Oh, Andrea—" Her mother hugged her hard. "Thank heaven Rick stopped that horrible man before he could hurt anyone else."

She shook her head. "I can hardly comprehend it. He doesn't care about himself."

"Of course he does! But it's his job!"

Andrea's anger suddenly got the better of her. "He could have died this morning, Mom!"

"*You* might have died if Rick hadn't intervened when he did."

"I don't want to talk about it. Let's get back to work. We have a lot to do."

Rick was finishing a cup of coffee in the loft's kitchen when he heard Andrea's footsteps on the stairs. Benton would have apprised her of the facts. In order not to alarm her, Rick walked over to the doorway so she'd notice him right away.

But maybe his surprise visit hadn't been such a good idea, he thought. The second those soulful blue eyes saw him, the color left her face. He knew about her fear. Because of that, he'd driven his car straight here from the hospital to reassure her nothing was wrong with him.

"Easy, Andrea."

Before she fainted, he picked her up in his

arms and carried her through to the bedroom, where he laid her on the bed. She stared up at him. "I—I thought you were still at the hospital," she whispered.

He leaned over her, smoothing some gold strands from her forehead. "Just long enough to be checked out and released." She was so enticing, he found her mouth and kissed her until she clung to him because she couldn't help herself.

When they came up for air, one of her hands strayed to his face. "Benton said the fire singed your hair and eyelashes, but it's not nearly as bad as I had imagined."

Rick kissed the palm. "I'm glad to hear it. You think Tessa will notice?"

"Yes. She notices everything. Little girls who love their fathers are like that." Tears trickled out of the corners of her eyes. "Thank goodness you weren't killed, Rick."

He lowered his mouth to hers in a gentler kiss. "It didn't come to that."

"How did you know what Chase was going to do?"

"Instead of dragging you back into the house and my bed last night, I used all my energy to concentrate on that devious mind of his. By coming to your shop, he made it too obvious he planned to set it on fire. Since he knew I was home recovering, what better time for him to do something to throw us off the track and plant a device in your car? Firebugs like to set cars on fire."

She clutched his hand. "You saved my life." Her voice shook. "How can I ever repay you?"

He studied the mouth he'd been devouring. This was where he wanted to stay for the rest of his life. "By stopping your worry. I've been told I can't report to work until Thursday, so I've decided a mini vacation is in order. Do you think the Gingerbread Inn would have rooms for us?"

Andrea sat up looking totally shocked. "It has a lot of rooms, but I couldn't possibly go there with you."

"Why not? Tessa can miss a day of school. Do you think your mother could spare you for that long? With the sun shining, we should take advantage of it and celebrate the good news about Chase's capture. We'll take turns driving to give both of us a rest. Along the way we'll stop for meals and return tomorrow."

When she averted her eyes, he got off the bed. "I know you planned never to see me again once this business was over. But I don't think going on a little outing with Tessa will do irreparable damage."

Andrea rolled onto her side and slid off the bed. "You're wrong, Rick. No one is more thrilled than I that you're safe, but I never plan to go through this experience again, and you know why."

There was still something she hadn't told him—his instincts sensed it.

"Obviously your answer is no, but that isn't a problem. It was just an idea. I can see your fear is debilitating and I put you on the spot without meaning to, so I'll say merry Christmas to you now and wish you a wonderful trip."

"What trip?"

"The one you're going to take to the south of Spain after Christmas. I hear it's warm and beautiful there this time of year."

"Mom told you?"

"She happened to be on the phone with your sister-in-law when I entered the shop. I understand you've been invited to join her and her husband after Christmas. After

you've gone, I have relatives coming for New
Year's. Tessa's world will be full of excitement with her cousins. I promise you she'll
be fine whether you come with us today or
not. It's your call."

Her lack of response poleaxed him, but
there was always the New Year when she
got back from Europe, because he refused
to give up. Struggling for control, he moved
to the doorway. He'd made a decision and
would stick to it.

Get out of here, Jenner.

"Goodbye, Andrea."

He raced down the steps and through the
shop. Her mother was waiting on a customer.
"Merry Christmas and happy New Year,
Mrs. Bernard."

Her gaze darted to him in surprise. "The
same to you, Captain Jenner. As I told you
earlier, words can't express all our gratitude
for what you've done for our family. We owe
you everything."

"Say no more. It goes with the territory."

Once outside, he levered himself into the
car and headed for Benton's house to pick up
his daughter. He needed her. Whatever they
ended up doing today, he didn't want to be

alone with his thoughts. Andrea kept fighting him. He'd thought by now he would have broken her down, but such wasn't the case.

There was a reason she'd been invited to Spain. No doubt her late husband's sister had picked out a man she wanted her to meet. A European whose occupation wouldn't threaten her and who had the approval of the Fleming family. Someone safe.

Rick's hands gripped the steering wheel tightly. No man could be immune to her beauty. The guys at the station couldn't stop talking about her. Neither could Benton. Chase had gotten sidetracked by it. Because of it he'd now be spending time in the hospital before he was sent to prison.

By the time he reached Benton's house it was noon. He went inside and discovered the children were finishing their lunch. After thanking Deanna profusely, he told her he was taking Tessa home with him for some daddy-daughter time. They went out to the car and he strapped her in before driving off.

"How come I don't have to go to school today, Daddy?"

"Because I miss you and want you home with me."

"I miss you *all* the time."

"You do?"

"Yes. Every time you go away, I'm afraid you won't come back."

Her words drove a pain deep into his gut. *Andrea's exact words about her father.*

When they reached the house and went inside, he carried her into the den and sat down with her. "Tessa? Will you tell me the truth about something?"

She gazed at him out of those beautiful green eyes, then touched his hair. "What happened? It looks funny right here."

Andrea had warned him his daughter would notice. "I got too close to a Christmas candle. It'll grow back."

His daughter's expression sobered. "Julie said you were in a bad fire and had to go to the hospital again. I was afraid you'd die like Mommy and I cried all morning."

Oh, hell. Benton's little girl had big ears and had probably listened in on her parents' conversations. Naturally she had told Tessa everything. "Well, as you can see, I'm fine."

"No, you're not. Your eyelashes look funny, too. I wish you didn't have to put out fires. Julie's daddy doesn't have to anymore. She says he's home a lot doing his work."

Tessa had never said these things to him before. "Does it worry you what I do, sweetheart?"

Her eyes filled with tears. Suddenly she slid off his lap and ran out of the room. Alarmed, he got up and followed her to the bedroom. She lay down on her stomach, parka and all. He watched her body heave with silent sobs.

"Tessa—look at me."

"I don't want to."

His dark brows furrowed. "Why?"

"Cos I'm afraid you're mad at me for saying that."

He knelt down. "I could never be mad at you. I love you."

"Promise?"

Heartsick over that question, he said, "Don't you know that already?"

She flung her body around and hugged his neck. "Please don't die, Daddy." Now her sobs were vocal. They held on to each other for a long time. Tessa clung to him until she'd cried out her tears and finally fell quiet.

His phone rang, disturbing the silence.

"Don't answer it, Daddy! Don't go to another fire!" The anxiety in her voice was terrifying to him. After the talk with Andrea, he realized how deep-seated his own daughter's fear had become since losing her mother.

How could he not have known? Though Tina hadn't been thrilled about what he did for a living, she'd never let it become an issue. But maybe she and Tessa had talked about it in private and Tina's death had brought their daughter's fear to the surface.

"I'm off duty, sweetheart, so I'm not going anywhere. I'll just see who it is." He pulled the cell from his pocket. The blood pounded in his ears. *Andrea.*

Whatever was on her mind, he didn't want to talk to her in front of Tessa. His daughter was already too upset. He let it ring, deciding to call her back when Tessa got busy doing something else. "It's not an important call," he lied. "What would you like to do today? I'll let you choose."

More animated, she jumped off the bed. "Can we go to Andrea's shop and look at the nutcrackers?"

His heart thundered in his chest. All roads led to Andrea. His daughter had just given him an excuse to find out what Andrea wanted. So much for his decision to leave her alone. "Why don't I call her and see if it will be all right?"

CHAPTER SEVEN

"THANK YOU. I'll be by for it later today."

Andrea got off the phone with the car rental agency and started out of the bedroom. On the way downstairs her cell rang. She checked the caller ID and immediately clicked on. "Rick?"

She knew she sounded out of breath. It had been ten minutes since she'd phoned him. When he hadn't answered, she'd feared she'd angered him beyond forgiveness. Taking her silence as a firm goodbye, he'd left the loft like a shot and she'd wanted to die. He'd just saved her life, and she'd let him go without saying a word!

"Are you all right?"

I am now. "Yes. Thank you for calling me back. You're a much better person than I am."

"What can I do for you?"

He *was* upset.

She leaned against the stair railing for support. "I—I've been thinking about what you said…." Her voice faltered. "Tessa has a whole fulfilling life with you, so being around me for another day isn't going to be the end of the world for her. As you told her, you and I are friends. You were right about something else, too. After almost losing your life this morning, we should celebrate. If you still want to drive to Barrow's Cove, I'd love to go."

"If you're saying this because you feel you owe me, I'd rather not see you again." His borderline wintry tone gutted her.

"I want to be with you," she admitted on a whisper. He would never know how much.

"That's all I needed to hear. Tessa and I will be in the alley in half an hour."

Excitement almost caused her to crush the phone in her hand. "Honk when you've arrived and I'll come out."

After hanging up, she hurried downstairs to tell her mother what was going on. Under the circumstances her mom decided to close the store for the rest of the day and go home. It was music to Andrea's ears that Rex would be going over there to inspect the damage in the garage and take her out to dinner.

Once upstairs again, Andrea phoned the car rental agency and told them she wouldn't be picking it up until later the next afternoon. All she needed to do now was pack her overnight bag and winter clothing.

On impulse she phoned the inn and spoke to Carol, who sounded delighted they were coming and said she would get a couple of rooms ready for them. When she asked who the man was, Andrea told her it was a friend. Carol let it go at that.

When Andrea heard the honk, she grabbed the pecan roll her mother had brought her and hurried out the door. Rick got out of the driver's seat at the same time. Their eyes met for a breathtaking moment before he put her things into the trunk. He'd forgiven her this time, but she knew her behavior could destroy any feelings he might have for her if she kept this up.

"Andrea—"

She knew that voice, and she climbed into the front seat before turning to his daughter. "Tessa—how are you, darling?"

"I'm glad you could come on a trip with us."

"So am I. It's kind of fun to miss a day of school."

She giggled for happiness. "Daddy says we're going to a lake where he used to water-ski."

"I used to go there, too. We'd boat and swim and have a wonderful time, but it's too cold to do that in winter. Years ago there was a place that took people sleigh riding around the lake in the snow. I've never done it, but maybe we could do it today before dinner."

"You mean like in Santa's sleigh?"

Rick darted Andrea a smiling glance.

"Exactly like that."

"With reindeer?"

He burst into deep laughter. "I think horses, sweetheart."

"We'll eat treats and see what kind of birds and little animals we can spot. There'll be a lot of them around the inn where we'll be staying."

"What's an inn?"

"It's another word for a hotel. My family used to spend our summers there. That's where I met my best friends. After we get settled, we'll go for a walk while your daddy takes a nap."

"He needs one. Did you know his hair got burned in the fire?"

"It did?" She pretended to know nothing.

"Yes, and his eyelashes."

She looked over at him. "He still looks good to me," she said to hide her emotions. Whether injured, sleep deprived or unshaven, Rick was still the most striking male anywhere around, bar none.

He grinned. "I think I like the sound of that."

Without snow or ice on the freeway, they made good time. When they came to the outskirts of Barrow's Cove, Rick pulled into a family restaurant. "I feel like some hot chili. Do I hear any takers?"

Andrea nodded. "That sounds delicious."

"I want a hot dog and a hot chocolate," Tessa proclaimed.

Before long they'd eaten and were on the road again. This made twice in one week Andrea had come here, but being with Rick and Tessa this time was so different and thrilling, she had to pinch herself to believe this was real.

Soon the small hand-painted sign with a

wooden arrow pointing up the hill announcing the inn came into view. There'd been no snowplows here. Part snow, part slush covered the gravel drive. Tessa was all eyes as Rick pulled to a stop near the sagging front wraparound porch.

"Is this a haunted house?"

Both Rick and Andrea burst into laughter. Trying to view the dilapidation and snow-covered tree limbs from a child's vantage point, she knew it did look forlorn with only Carol's pickup parked at the side.

"No, darling. It's a place loaded with happy memories. But the owner can't take care of it anymore and is trying to sell it, so that's why it looks a little sad. But you'll find it cozy and charming inside."

Rick got the bags out and they climbed the porch stairs. To Tessa's delight the golden retriever came running out the front door and started sniffing her. "This is Harper, Carol's dog. She's very friendly."

Carol met them in the foyer and hugged her. "How lucky am I to see you again so soon!"

"I feel the same way. Carol Parsons, I want you to meet two very important people. Rick

Jenner and his daughter, Tessa, from Providence. She's in kindergarten and Rick is a firefighter for the Providence Fire Department."

The older woman beamed at them. "You can climb up the ladder to my window any time," she teased, causing him to laugh. "Young lady? Did you know you're my first customers today, but I'm expecting some more guests later. Welcome to the Gingerbread Inn!"

"Gingerbread?" Tessa's squeal reverberated through the hallway, causing the three of them to chuckle. "Does the Gingerbread Man live here?"

Rick tousled her blond curls. His dashing smile turned Andrea's heart over. "Who knows? After he ran away, maybe the fox didn't eat him after all and he decided to hide here."

"Daddy...you're funny."

"When the inn was built, they called it that to let guests know it was children friendly."

"It was always a magical place to me, Carol."

Tessa's green eyes twinkled. "Santa Claus is going to bring me a gingerbread man."

"He is?" Carol clapped her hands together. "That's right! Christmas will be here before we know it. Do you want to follow me up the stairs to your rooms?"

"Come on, Daddy." While Tessa trudged on up the old-fashioned staircase with Carol and the dog, Andrea reached for her overnight bag. Rick brought the rest.

"I've put you in the rose room and the Jenners are across the hall in the lilac room." Each room had two double beds, all of them four-posters with chintz quilts.

Tessa walked in to look around. "Did you used to sleep in here, Andrea?"

"With Casey, Melissa and Emily. We had a slumber party every night."

"I don't think they slept much," Carol said with a laugh. "They stayed up half the night gabbing." Rick sent her another private, heart-grabbing smile.

"We're going on a sleigh ride!"

Carol eyed Tessa ruefully. "If you're talking about Sterling's, they're not doing that sleigh ride anymore. It's a shame, but these are hard times."

Andrea's spirits plummeted for Tessa's

sake. "Oh well, we're going to have lots of fun anyway, aren't we, Tessa?"

She nodded her cute blond head. The dog had engaged her attention, which was a good thing. Clearly Tessa was so happy being out with her daddy, nothing else mattered to her.

"Make yourselves comfortable. If there's anything you need, come and find me in the kitchen. I've got fresh coffee and coffee cake for you. If you get hungry in the night, just rummage in the kitchen all you want."

"You're too good to be true, Mrs. Parsons."

"Call me Carol."

Andrea hugged her. "You're an angel."

After she disappeared, Andrea walked across the worn carpet to the other bedroom. "I bet your father is sleepy. Shall we let him lie down while you and I take a walk around the inn?"

"Yes. You go to bed, Daddy. You need your sleep."

Rick didn't put up a fight. After what he'd lived through over the past few days, Andrea knew he needed rest more than anything. "Thank you." He mouthed the words to her before she left with Tessa.

Andrea could see his exhaustion was so great, he might sleep longer than a few hours. In anticipation, she talked to Tessa about going for a long walk by the lake instead. His daughter was willing to go along with anything.

As it turned out, Rick didn't wake up till the next morning. After their walk with Harper, Andrea and Tessa ate dinner in the kitchen with Carol. They talked about the plans for the wedding-vows party and how they would decorate. Then they sat in front of the fire to eat coffee cake for dessert. Carol brought out an old puzzle, which they all worked on until it was time to go to bed. Andrea kept Tessa in her own room so Rick wouldn't be disturbed.

At four in the morning, Rick came wide awake. He raised himself up in bed and saw that Tessa's bed hadn't been slept in. Once again he'd slept a solid twelve hours.

Unable to lie there anymore, he got up to shower and shave. The long uninterrupted sleep had made him feel like a new man. If he didn't suspect his daughter was asleep in Andrea's room, he'd go in and make love to the beautiful woman—the woman who had stolen his heart—until the sun streamed through the windows.

Barring that, he had to do something with all this energy. He decided to take Carol up on her offer and raid the kitchen before he took a walk outside in the snow. Between heavy conversations with Andrea and Tessa, he had a lot of serious thinking to do about his life and where he wanted to go from here.

One thing he knew beyond all else. He couldn't imagine a life that didn't include Andrea. The idea of her leaving for Spain after Christmas was unthinkable to him.

It was six-thirty when he returned to the inn and went up the stairs. After removing his boots and parka, he slipped across the hall to Andrea's room. The two people he loved most in the world were still sleeping peacefully. He hunkered down at the side of the bed.

"Andrea?" he whispered.

She stirred and opened her eyes. Heavens, she was beautiful. Then she sat up in alarm. "Rick—is something wrong with Tessa?"

It thrilled him that her concern for his daughter was at the forefront of her mind.

He couldn't fall in love with a woman who didn't love his daughter as much as possible. He knew Andrea did.

Taking precautions, he put a finger to her lips. "She's still out for the count. I need to talk to you alone. This is important. Come across to my room. We'll leave both doors open. If she wakes up, she'll know where we are."

Her eyes wandered over him. "You're already dressed."

"I woke up early and took a walk outside."

She took an audible breath. "I need to put on some clothes."

"I'll wait for you in my room." Rick pressed a kiss to the base of her throat before he left. He stood at his window and looked out at the lake until she joined him wearing jeans and a becoming plum-colored sweater. With her golden hair, she looked fantastic in everything. "Come over here by me."

"I'm afraid to."

"That's honest. By now you know I'd like to eat you alive, and that's just for starters."

She stayed where she was in the center of the room, rubbing her palms against womanly hips. "You sound like you must be feeling better."

"I feel reborn."

"I wish twelve hours' sleep would do the same thing for me."

"Frankly it wasn't the sleep that turned me around. Although I admit I needed it and appreciate you taking care of Tessa."

"She's a joy. To be truthful, she took care of me."

"Tina and I often remarked she was going to make a good little mother one day." He eyed her for a long moment. "You're going to be a wonderful mother in the future, too. I can imagine your children decked out in little alpine outfits." He'd almost said *our* children. "It's no secret Tessa likes you more and more every day. What would it take to prevent you from going on that trip to Spain?"

Maybe it was a trick of light, but he thought she paled a little. "Why do you ask?"

"I thought the reason was obvious."

She clutched the back of the nearest chair. "I've already told you this little celebration outing has to be the end for me."

"I can't accept that. The last thing I want is for you to leave Providence." He moved closer. "If I had my way, we'd spend every moment together with no separations."

She lifted her chin. "Except for when you're fighting fires, or recovering in the hospital, *or* sleeping twelve hours at a time to recuperate before you tempt death again. I care for you very much, Rick, and care what happens to you. In fact, there are no words to tell you what I really think of you."

"Then show me instead," he begged as his mouth descended. He needed her kiss more than he needed breath.

"Rick—" she cried against his lips before she began kissing him back with an urgency that set him on fire. He drew them over to the bed and followed her down, desperately hungry for her. They lay entwined, trying without success to subdue the desire exploding inside them.

"I want you in my life, Andrea. Can't you see I've fallen in love with you?" He looked down at her, cupping her hot cheeks. "Admit you've fallen in love with me, too."

A moan escaped her lips. "I don't dare."

"That's because you *are* in love. Don't be cruel and shut me out. I couldn't take it."

She rolled her head away from him. "But

I couldn't take living in fear again like I did throughout my childhood."

"You don't have to."

Her head jerked back. With blazing eyes she looked up at him. "What are you saying?"

He kissed her lips quiet. "I've made a decision that will put you and Tessa out of your misery."

She frowned. "I—I don't understand," she stammered. "Why do you mention Tessa in the same breath?"

"Yesterday my daughter and I had a heart-to-heart. You told me she would notice my singed hair and lashes. You were right. Then she bared her soul to me. I learned she's been living in fear of what I do for a living every time I walk out the door. I heard *you* in her, Andrea."

"Oh, no—"

"It was a revelation. I saw and felt it, and I was devastated. One day I live in fear that she'll accuse me of loving my work more than I love her."

Andrea caressed his cheek. "She would never do that, because she knows how much you love her. You're devoted to her every second that you're home. That wasn't the case with my father. He didn't like to be home and didn't want me. Don't ever compare yourself to him."

Pained, yet loving her for saying that, he pressed another kiss to her luscious mouth before he sat up. "But maybe love isn't enough if her fear grows too great. I've thought about nothing else since she told me."

"Has she asked you to stop?"

"Not in those words. What she did say was, 'Please don't die, Daddy.'"

Andrea sat up and looped her arms around his neck. "That must have killed you."

He rubbed her back, pulling her closer. "It did. I always thought Tina was straight up with me. We got lined up on a blind date after I became a firefighter. She knew why I wanted to be one, but I think deep inside she must have hated it, too, and somehow Tessa picked up on it. All this time she has held back...until yesterday."

"The little darling."

"While I was outside walking earlier, I had an epiphany. You wouldn't know, but for the last year Benton has been asking me to consider coming to work for the arson squad."

"That goes along with what he said," she murmured.

"What do you mean?"

"Yesterday he told me you had remarkable, exceptional instincts for that kind of work. Does this mean you'd give up firefighting altogether?"

Rick shouldn't have been surprised at the wonder in her expression. "Yes, but it would still let me be a part of a world I love—just a different aspect of it."

"What would you actually do?"

"As you found out with Chase, a fire that is caused deliberately with malicious intent to cover up another crime, or to collect insurance money on the property, is arson. I would become an arson investigator and inspect fire sites full-time to determine what exactly caused the fire, and if the fire was set intentionally. If it appears to be arson rather than an accident, my job will be to figure out where in the house or building the fire started and what was used to start it."

"Then there's no danger involved?"

"None at all. You gather evidence, communicate with law enforcement, write reports and testify in court as a witness."

"You'll still be helping people."

"Yes." He kissed her mouth again.

"But it won't be like fighting fires, something you've always wanted to do." Her eyes bored deep into his soul. "Would it be hard for you to give it up? I know why you fight fires, and it might be asking too much of you."

"Not when in exchange I'm going to make you and my daughter happy. That means more to me than anything else."

She bowed her head. "When are you going to tell Tessa?"

"After I've spoken to Benton and turned in my resignation."

"Your superiors are going to mourn their loss."

"My leaving will give some other guy a chance to do what he loves."

"How soon will you speak to them?"

"I'll phone Benton today to get the process started. I'm fully aware Tessa needs to hear my decision right away so she can stop worrying."

"Your news will change her whole life."

"And what about your life?" He smoothed

the hair off her cheek. "I want to know how *you* feel about what I've just told you."

Andrea eased off the bed. The act itself caused him some consternation. "My feelings shouldn't matter, Rick. I don't want to be one of the reasons you're considering making this huge career move. I feel so responsible already, I think I'm frightened."

Rick's brows knit together. He got to his feet. "Something's wrong. What aren't you telling me?"

She clasped her hands nervously. "If I weren't in the picture—if I hadn't told you about my fears because of my father—would you honestly be reading this much into Tessa's fear? Maybe with some therapy she could go on handling what you do."

Her reaction was the last thing Rick had anticipated. Perplexed, he rubbed the back of his neck. "I thought you and I were in the same place emotionally, but I sense that we're not. Even having told you what I'm prepared to do, your reaction leaves me baffled. What I'm concluding is that all along things have been sketchy with you and they still are. I can see our relationship has been too much for you this soon after Gunter."

"No, Rick—that's not true." She sounded panicked.

"I think it is. I went through my mourning for a long time while Tina was still alive and am evidently ready to move on. But you lost your husband in an accident and are still grieving because it happened so quickly. I've been trying to make something work between us you're not ready for. Maybe you never will be."

She let out a sigh of exasperation. "If I didn't feel something powerful for you, do you think I would have gone to the hospital to see if you were all right?"

"I think you were acting on hormones that had suddenly kicked in. As you said, physical attraction can be very strong without involving the emotions. You've been missing your husband and wanted to feel alive again after so much pain. But it's evident you can't make a move that will constitute a commitment of any kind yet. You're simply not there."

"Rick—please listen to me."

"It's not your fault." He bit out the words. "It's mine for wanting something so badly. I'll get over it, but let's not drag this out."

"Don't you know you're going to meet other wom—"

"Spare me the speech." He cut her off. "I don't want to hear about some fictitious female who's going to come into my life and transform it and how we'll be perfect for each other. I've had enough of that from friends and family. But I don't want to hear it from you of all people."

Before he lost it completely, he moved past her to go wake up his daughter. Andrea hurried after him. When they reached the hall, she grasped his arm. "You've got things wrong."

Rick spun around, forcing her to let go. "No. Otherwise you'd be telling me what I want to hear. Let's agree you're taking this trip to Spain to get away from me. Though it isn't necessary, because I don't intend to be with you again after today. I can see that's why you're leaving. I should have known something this marvelous was too good to be true."

As he turned, he was shocked to discover Tessa standing in the doorway to her room, still in her nightgown. She was all eyes. "What's wrong, Daddy?"

"Nothing, sweetheart. We were just talking." He gave her a kiss.

"But you said Andrea was going away."

The truth, Jenner. "Not today. Later on she's going to spend some time with her husband's family."

"When are you going to leave?"

"After Christmas," he answered for her. "Come on. Let's get you dressed. After we eat breakfast we're going to go back and see the ice sculptures at the university on the way home. I understand they have some Disney characters you'll love."

To his relief Andrea had disappeared for the moment to give them some private time. But Tessa wasn't listening to him. She'd focused on Andrea and wouldn't let go. "I don't want her to go."

"I'm sorry." He walked her into the room to help her get dressed. "But we're going to have your grandma and grandpa at our house. And Uncle John's family and your cousins Lizzy and Jake."

Her lower lip quivered, a dead giveaway she was on the verge of tears. After she put on her pants and top, he helped her on with her boots. "Listen to me, Tessa. She's been our friend and we've been having a great time. But she misses her husband's sister and this is her chance to visit her."

"What if she doesn't come back?"

Her question acted like a vise squeezing his lungs. "Of course she'll come back. She works in the shop with her mother. Tessa, let's just be happy she's spending today with us. It won't be long before I have to drop her off at work and take you to school."

"I don't want to go to kindergarten today."

"But you missed yesterday." He finished packing up her things. "Julie will be glad you're back. No tears, now." He picked her up. "If you'll give me a kiss, I'll tell you a secret."

Though his sweet little girl was unhappy, she gave him a big one on the cheek. "What is it?"

This couldn't wait. He was desperate to help her out of her pain. "I'm not going to be a firefighter anymore."

She stared at him for the longest time. "You're not?"

"No. When we go home I'm telling Benton that I'm going to work with him on the arson squad. I won't be riding a truck anymore, so you don't ever have to worry about me again. But you can't tell anyone yet. Not even Julie."

Tears of joy welled in her big green eyes. She wrapped her arms around his neck so hard she almost cut off his breathing. Andrea had done the same thing to him earlier, though not for the same reason.

"Can I tell Andrea?"

"She already knows." But for some underlying reason he didn't understand, his decision had made no difference to her.

Once Rick had paid the bill and Andrea had thanked Carol for everything, they took off. Andrea offered to drive, but he told her he felt rested and wanted to do it, so she didn't insist. Tessa asked a lot of questions about her upcoming trip to Spain until he turned on the radio to a station that played Christmas music.

He drove them past the amazing sculptures and stopped for lunch, after which he headed for the shop. When he parked in the alley, Andrea got out and opened the back door to say goodbye to Tessa.

"I hope you had as wonderful a time as

I did. I'll be thinking of you-know-what on Christmas morning."

In the rearview mirror he could see his daughter's green eyes. They stayed dry. She was being the best little soldier in the world and he was proud of her. As for Rick, he was the one who was dying inside.

"Do you promise Santa will bring me the gingerbread man?"

"I know he will. Now, have a lovely day at school." She leaned in to give her a kiss on the cheek. "Oh, I forgot." She reached into her purse. "This is some candy my mother made for you and your daddy. It's really good." Andrea handed it to her. "Merry Christmas."

As she stood up, Rick was there with her overnight bag. She reached for the remote on her keys to open the back door. He followed her inside. Her mother was probably out on the floor. There was no sign of her. Andrea turned to him.

She couldn't look him in the eye. "Thank you for the outing. Thank you for everything…for saving my life," she whispered.

"Anytime. Have a safe flight to Spain."

He was out the door before he made the grave mistake of crushing her in his arms one more time.

CHAPTER EIGHT

SEVERAL DAYS LATER Andrea got her sister-in-law on the phone. *Please answer.*

"Marie?"

"Andrea—it's wonderful to hear your voice. I can't wait for you to come to Spain with us so we can have a long talk."

She gripped her phone tighter. "That's why I'm calling. I—I can't come." Her voice faltered.

"What's wrong?"

"I hope this won't come as a shock to you, but I've met a man."

"It's about time," Marie responded without hesitation. "I hope you're going to tell me you're in love."

Tears welled in her eyes. "I am. Terribly."

"I've prayed this would happen to you."

"He's not like Gunter. Rick's a firefighter

who lost his wife. His little daughter, Tessa, has captured my heart, but there's one big problem."

"Has he asked you to marry him?"

"Yes. He even said he was giving up fire-fighting for me and Tessa so we wouldn't worry about him anymore. But just a little while ago I ended it with him."

"Why?"

"He doesn't know I can't have children."

"If you truly love him, then you have to go to him and face your demons. Talk to him about what happened to you in the accident. It's not up to you to decide how he'll react and feel. You're so certain he'll reject you for being unable to have children. But don't you see you're denying him his agency to choose what he wants for himself? That's wrong!"

"Mother told me virtually the same thing." *You could be passing up a great love affair out of fear.*

"Let's put this another way. What if Rick wouldn't commit to you because he couldn't give you a child? Consider how you feel about him right now. If he avoided being with you for the same reason, how would you react?"

"But it's not the same thing!"

"Of course it is! How can you say that?"

"Because he had plans to enlarge his family and deserves to find a woman who can give him another child."

"Just listen to yourself, Andrea. He may have had plans, but his wife died. *You* had plans, too, but Gunter died. It's life! If both of you want children, then adoption would be the route to go. At least give him the chance to tell you whether it's what he wants or not. He's already told you he's going to give up firefighting to win your love."

"But—"

"But what? Are you really afraid he'll reject you? He's not your father, Andrea," she inserted quietly.

"What do you mean?"

"Gunter once confided in me about him and how much damage he did to you. I can see you're afraid that in the end, Rick won't want you enough."

Andrea closed her eyes for a moment. Marie had hit on the crux of her greatest fear.

"If I were you, I'd prove myself right or wrong. But if you can't, then maybe you should get professional help. Otherwise you'll go through this every time you meet a man who wants a relationship with you. If that happens, you'll be single all your life. Is that what you really want—because that's where you're headed. Gunter would say the same thing, and you know it."

Marie was so right about everything, Andrea couldn't find the words. "Thank you for being my dearest friend and setting me straight. I'll love you forever. Take care of yourself. I promise I'll call and let you know what happens."

"I'll be waiting."

After Andrea hung up, she started rehearsing what she'd say to Rick. There was only one more call to make. The most important one of her life.

What if he didn't want to see or talk to her again? She was terrified of his response. When she called his house, Sharon answered and said he'd gone downtown to a special meeting, but she'd make sure he got the message that she'd called.

When Rick left department headquarters, Benton was waiting for him outside the public safety building in downtown Providence. The chief and battalion commander had held an impromptu goodbye party for him. Some of the guys had come in and there'd been a lot of laughs, but now it was over.

"Ready to go home? There's more partying to be had at my house."

Rick eyed his best friend. "I know."

"Tessa's one happy little girl."

Yes. She's happy except for one thing. After losing her mother, she was suffering over a second loss.

"How does it feel to be a free man?"

As of today he was no longer a firefighter. "First tell me I have a job with you, then I'll respond."

"Was there ever any doubt?" He squeezed his shoulder. "Welcome to the dark side." Benton could be a tease. The ironic term had been coined because it was the arson squad that unearthed the dark matter after a fire to learn the cause. "I'm having your name printed on the door of your new office." It would take Rick a while to get used to it. "You don't have to start until January 2."

"I owe you for so many things, Benton, I hardly know where to start."

"Don't go sappy on me now. I seem to recall an incident five years ago where you saved my life before I was promoted to the arson unit. Deanna still cries about it. Sometimes I think she loves you more than she loves me."

"You're full of it."

"I just wanted you to remember I've owed you for a long time."

They walked to the parking lot. Rick had left his car at the Ames house and ridden downtown with Benton. Because of his change of career, his plans had changed. He'd decided to take advantage of the next ten days off and spend them with his family in Cranston. He and Tessa would stay at his parents' home while Sharon got a well-earned rest at her brother's.

Tonight after Tessa went to bed he'd load all the presents into the car. In the morning they'd drive over to see Tina's parents and spend some time with them. Later in the day they'd head out for Cranston. With four cousins under the age of eight, his daughter would have a whole week to enjoy them. Hopefully in that amount of time she'd be able to face going to school again.

Tessa had become attached to Andrea and

it showed. Maybe being with family would make a difference.

From the entrance to the circle Rick could see at least a dozen cars parked. A little closer and he glimpsed the painted banner across the front of Benton's house. "Congratulations on your promotion, Investigator Jenner!"

His eyes smarted.

Before Benton had pulled up in the driveway, the children came running outside. Rick jumped from the car as soon as he could and swept his daughter into his arms.

"Are you all through fighting fires, Daddy?"

"All through, sweetheart."

All through.

They went inside, where he was besieged by more congratulations from the men and families with whom he'd worked the most closely over the years. The celebrating continued until nine-thirty when Rick could see his daughter was conking out fast. With his plan to drive to Cranston tomorrow, he decided he needed to get her home to bed. He still had a lot to do after she fell asleep.

With profuse thanks to Benton and Deanna for all they had done, he gathered Tessa and they drove home. For once she fell asleep the moment her head touched the pillow. The knowledge that he wouldn't be fighting any more fires had something to do with her being able to relax. But twice during the party she'd mentioned that she wished Andrea had been there with them.

Andrea was never out of his daughter's mind. *Or his.*

After getting half a dozen big garbage bags from the kitchen pantry, he packed up the presents under the tree and went out to the garage to fill the trunk. Everyone had gone overboard out of love for his daughter, but there was an indecent amount of gifts.

In a few minutes he headed for the basement to bring up the presents he'd hidden from her. Those he put on the backseat of the car and covered with some blankets. All that was left was the big carton from Santa Claus, which he brought upstairs to the kitchen. He hoped it would fit in the backseat with the rest of the gifts; otherwise he'd have to open it.

Rick hated undoing it, because Andrea had wrapped it so beautifully. The vision of how she'd looked at the station when she'd delivered it had never left his mind. While he stood there aching for her, he spotted the note Sharon had left under the fridge magnet before she'd gone to her brother's house.

Hardly able to breathe, he pulled out his cell and phoned Andrea.

"Rick?"

His heart almost failed him. "I just got Sharon's message."

"Forgive me for calling. I-if you don't want to talk to me, just hang up and I'll never bother you again. I swear it."

A surge of adrenaline charged his body. "Where are you?"

"Home."

He gripped the phone tighter. "What's wrong?"

"Look, if this is a bad time, please tell me. I realize I could be interrupting anything. If Tessa is nearby, I don't want her to know I'm on the phone."

"I put her to bed a half hour ago," he answered, still in a daze.

"I need to talk to you, th-that is if you're willing."

His heart was getting the workout of its life. "Are you at your mother's or the apartment?"

"The apartment."

"I'd come over there, but Sharon has gone to her brother's until after New Year's."

"Does that mean you're leaving Providence?" Unless he was mistaken, she didn't sound happy about it.

"Tomorrow we're headed for my parents in Cranston to stay the week."

"Then this is a bad time to be calling. We can talk again after you're back from your trip. Your family must be thrilled you're coming." The throb in her voice was telling.

"I don't want to wait ten days to see you. Why don't you drive over here now?"

"You're one man who needs his sleep, Rick."

"But you're no longer speaking to Captain Jenner who has just come off shift and needs twelve hours to restore him."

A small cry escaped on the other end. "What are you saying?"

"What do you think?"

"So you really resigned? It's all over?"

He took a fortifying breath. "As of today I'm officially known as Investigator Jenner of the Providence Arson Squad. Benton is already having my name put on the door of my new office in the department of public safety building." Might as well tell her everything right now.

"From now on I work several ten-hour shifts in one week, then I have two weeks off to do follow-up and paper work. One week I'm on call to do investigations. All of it safe."

"Oh, Rick—" Her cry resounded over the phone line. That was pure happiness he heard in her voice. "Tessa must be overjoyed."

"Yes." At least in that regard his daughter was at peace. As for himself, he would be a walking time bomb until he heard what she had to say. "Can you drive over right now?"

"But aren't you getting ready for bed?"

"Do you honestly think I could sleep after hearing your voice, knowing you're home?"

"What were you doing when I phoned?"

"Loading the ton of gifts for Tessa in my car. I'm still wondering how to get the big gift from Santa Claus inside. It might not fit. Come and help me."

"If you're sure."

His breath caught. "Why don't you come and find out?"

"I—I'll leave now." She sounded jittery. "I'm driving a rental car."

"I'll watch for you. For your information, I checked on your car. It's all repaired and ready for you to pick up at your convenience."

"That's great news. Thank you. I'll see you shortly."

"Drive carefully."

"You don't have to tell me that." Her voice sounded unusually shaky.

He'd said it automatically, but then he remembered her husband's fatal car accident.

Rick was on the porch waiting for Andrea when she pulled into his driveway. In the light she could see he was wearing a navy crewneck sweater with jeans. His tall, dark, handsome looks worked like an assault on her senses. It seemed like years since she'd last seen him. The pain of longing to be in his arms again reached the palms of her hands.

As he walked toward her, she realized he truly was the most wonderful, marvelous man alive. More than ever she dreaded what she had to tell him. But as Marie had said, Andrea needed to hear his response—otherwise she'd remain in a frozen state for the rest of her life, unable to go forward.

She got out of the car before he could help her. Andrea didn't want him touching her yet. As soon as she got inside the house, she took off her coat and put it on one of the living-room chairs.

He shut the door and walked slowly toward her, his hands in his pockets. Between his fire-singed black lashes, his hazel gaze traveled over her. After a shower at the apartment she'd decided to wear a new outfit he hadn't seen before—a lighter aqua top shot with gold threads and push-up sleeves to the elbow. The darker aqua skirt was made of the same silk jersey fabric.

"Did you know in the lights from the Christmas tree your hair gleams like the gold in your top? You look fabulous, Andrea."

"You look good, too. Rested."

Rick cocked his head and stood with his powerful legs slightly apart. "I take it something has happened you felt you had to discuss with me, if only for Tessa's sake. So tell me what it is, because I can't take the suspense any longer. I've never been a patient man."

Rick looked dark and dangerous right now, as if all his energy was barely sheathed. It sent shivers through her body.

"Let's sit down." She purposely chose one of the upholstered chairs.

He studied her for an overly long moment before he lounged against the arm of the couch. "Go on. This had better be important, after telling me you didn't intend to see me again." His voice sounded deeper than usual, almost gravelly.

"It is. Very." *Just say it, Andrea.* She was keeping him up and it wasn't fair to him, but the blood pounded in her ears. She couldn't sit still and jumped up. "I need to tell you about Gunter's accident."

Lines suddenly marred his striking features. He watched her pace until she stopped. His black brows rose. "Are you sure you want to talk about this?"

"I *have* to. H-he wasn't the only person in it."

His hands came out of his pockets. "Did another family member die, too?"

She shook her head. "*I* was the other person in the crash."

His sharp intake of breath resounded in the room. "You never told me that."

"I'm sorry I couldn't talk about it until now. I don't remember it, but I was told that another car on the freeway came at us out of nowhere. Apparently the police thought I was dead, because they had to pry me out to get to me."

Rick's color seemed to go gray. *"Andrea—"*

"When I woke up in a hospital room, I thought I had to be dreaming. IVs were hooked up to me. I remember Gunter's whole family surrounding me. His parents were too devastated to talk. It was Marie who told me we'd been in a bad accident and my husband had been killed outright.

"At first I couldn't comprehend it because I was so drugged. Mother arrived. It was then I realized I was awake and had lived through a horror story. But there was more. After a few days when I could get up and walk, Mom told me that the accident had caused internal injuries to my pelvis."

She swallowed hard before she admitted the one thing she feared telling Rick. "Mom told me I was operated on and would never be able to have children. That blow on top of losing my beloved husband was like being given a death sentence. I wanted to die, but of course I didn't."

Rick's face was a study in pain before he wrapped his arms around her. He held her for a long time before she lifted her head. "Would you believe that when my father called several weeks after I'd been home, he said that unlike Frank I'd dodged a bullet and was lucky I could walk. So I should get over it. At the time I hated him for it, but with hindsight it's probably the only good piece of advice he ever gave me."

"Andrea," he whispered in a pained voice against her neck before pressing kisses all over her face and hair.

"On some level I realized he was right. I was still alive and I needed to live for my mother's sake. Before long I discovered I needed to live for my own. That's when I decided to have the upstairs of the shop remodeled into an apartment and move in. My friends came to see me and I started getting out.

"I'd been doing pretty well until the day I saw you in front of the shop window holding Tessa. She was so dear, I moved closer to get a good look. Your daughter was the living version of my fantasy child I'd hoped to have one day with Gunter.

"You were so sweet to her as you both looked at everything. I thought then what a remarkable daddy you were to take her shopping, something my father never did with me. I saw this tall, attractive man enjoying a day out with his daughter and wondered what it would be like to get to know you. I couldn't stop staring. That's when you suddenly noticed me. Then your demeanor changed."

Rick molded her shoulders with his hands before he moved her far enough so he could look into her eyes. "That morning I was at my lowest ebb after doing all right for a long time. But the display had drawn me in, reminding me of happier times.

"When I saw this beautiful blonde woman watching us through the glass, instead of ignoring you I wanted to go on staring. At that moment I felt such a strong attraction, it angered me. Here I'd been thinking about Tina, and all of a sudden I was thinking about you. That hadn't happened to me since her death."

"We both had similar guilt reactions, Rick, and my feelings for you continued to grow despite any pitiful efforts on my part to avoid you. If anything, all I did was pursue you. I'm ashamed of myself when I look back."

His hands tightened on her upper arms. "Ashamed?"

"Well, embarrassed anyway."

"That makes two of us. On the day of the fire inspection, I sent Jose into your shop, but I couldn't stay away and went in there myself afterward. Your mother looked familiar to me and I discovered why when I found out you were her daughter. At that point, I couldn't stay away any longer.

"The truth is, I fell hard for you, Andrea Fleming. So did my daughter. I'm glad you've told me everything. So now does this mean you're going to marry me? I want you for my wife more than anything in this world."

With the mention of that word she eased away from him and moved over to the chair to steady herself. "Didn't you hear what I told you?"

He frowned. "I heard everything."

"But if we were to get married, I couldn't give you a child. Not ever."

"Are you saying we couldn't have a sex life?"

Heat rushed into her cheeks. "No. But I no longer have a uterus."

"We don't need it. I'll be able to make love to you morning, noon and night and never worry about your getting pregnant. Do you know how heavenly that sounds?"

She laughed in spite of the seriousness of the situation. "Darling—"

"Ah…I've been waiting for you to call me that. Every time you say it to Tessa I get jealous. Speaking of my daughter, we already have a child. She loves you, Andrea," he said calmly. "As for more children, when we want more, we'll put in for adoption so Tessa doesn't grow up a spoiled, pampered only child. I know a person at the state agency who can help us when the time comes."

Her eyes glazed over. "Be serious, Rick."

He rubbed the back of his neck, something he did when he was in deep thought. "Is this the reason you left? You thought I wouldn't want you?"

She twisted her hands. "I didn't know."

"You can't be serious. It's *you* I want to spend the rest of my life with." His eyes glittered with desire. "There's a hell of a lot you still don't know about me. Come here."

She needed no urging as he pulled her to the couch and lay down with her.

"How about a proper greeting for a man who's been dying of love for you?"

Time faded away as they gave in to their needs and began giving each other pleasure beyond imagining.

Some time later he whispered, "Admit your sister-in-law planned to introduce you to some man while you were gone."

She kissed his jaw. "That's absurd. There is no other man and never will be again."

"Thank heaven you said that. Now that I've got you exactly where I want you, I need to make total love to you, darling. But not where Tessa could walk in on us. You *are* going to marry me?"

"Yes!"

"Good. Now that we've got that out of the way, it had better be soon. I don't care about convention. I'd marry you tonight if we could."

"So would I, but I thought you'd never ask."

"Now she tells me." He barked with laughter.

"I needed to hear it because no other woman

is going to get a chance to snare you. You're mine."

"I don't want another woman." His smile melted her bones. "Santa brought me what I wanted for Christmas. Give me your mouth, Andrea. It's life to me, just as you are."

CHAPTER NINE

RICK WOKE UP at six with Andrea half lying on top of him, her head nestled beneath his chin. With her return he'd gotten his Christmas present early.

She was still sound asleep. He studied every beautiful feature. Her skin showed a tiny rash from his beard. He loved the way her hair fanned out like spun gold against the cushion. While she slept, he had an idea. Easing away from her, he crept over to the fireplace. After opening the flue, he put a match to the newspaper and kindling. Pretty soon they'd have a roaring fire to warm up the living room for her.

No telling when Tessa would wake up. Before she came running in, he went out to the kitchen and brought Andrea's gift for her into the living room. He set it right in front of the tree. It was conspicuous any time, but especially so without the other presents.

So far, so good.

He slipped his shoes back on and walked down the hall to his bedroom. He pulled a little wrapped package out of the drawer, along with another small ring box, and put them in his pocket. Then he tiptoed into Tessa's bedroom. This was going to be fun. The most fun he'd had since before Tina had been diagnosed with her fatal illness.

Unable to wait any longer, he sat down on the side of her bed and kissed her cheek. She stirred and opened her eyes. "Daddy!"

"Good morning, sweetheart."

She sat right up. A couple of blond curls flounced over her eyes. "Is it time to go to Cranston?"

"Not for a while. I came in here to tell you that we had a very special visitor come down the chimney last night."

Her eyes widened. "But it's not Christmas!"

"That's true, but when Santa Claus found out we wouldn't be here on Christmas, he came early to bring you your presents."

He heard her suck in her breath. "My gingerbread man?"

"I don't know. You'll have to open your present first."

She scrambled out of bed in her nightgown and ran through the hall to the living room. "How did he get such a big box down the chimney?" She hadn't seen Andrea yet. He'd placed the couch facing the fire.

Rick grinned. "He has his magic ways."

On the periphery he saw Andrea stir and sit up to see what was going on. Beneath her disheveled gold hair, her eyes dazzled like blue jewels. They exchanged a private glance. He put a finger to his lips. She smiled and waited.

"Go ahead and open it."

Having been given permission, she undid the ribbon and tore the paper. It took her a minute to get the job done. "I can't undo the lid, Daddy."

"I'll help you."

Winking at Andrea, he leaned over and pulled off the top. Both presents were wrapped in green and red tissue paper. Andrea had gone all out. He pulled out the chair first and set it down on the carpet. Tessa was jumping up and down with excitement.

"There. Now you can open it."

His daughter peeled away the paper, and there sat the carved rocking chair she'd sat in at the shop. "Get out the other present, Daddy. Hurry!"

With a deep chuckle, he pulled it out. She tore off the paper faster than a whirlwind could do it. "He brought me my gingerbread man!" She squealed in such delight it brought tears to his eyes. "Andrea promised he would."

When he looked at the woman responsible for such happiness, tears were running down her cheeks. Together they watched his daughter sit down in the chair and cuddle her gift as if it were the most precious baby on earth.

"Santa Claus brought you something else, too."

The rocking stopped and she looked up at him. "What?"

"Do you remember what you said during your prayers last night? You wished Andrea weren't going away?"

"Yes?"

"Why don't you look over on the couch?"

Tessa got up with her treasure to see. "Andrea— you came back!"

"Yes, darling."

All the joy in the world exploded from his daughter. She ran over and flung herself into Andrea's arms, gingerbread man and all. Quickly before he broke down from too much emotion, Rick pulled out his phone and took a picture of the two of them embracing like mother and daughter. Before much longer, they *would* be.

"I'm going to get my gingerbread book." She dashed out of the room and was back in another instant. "Here it is."

"Shall we read it?"

"Yes."

"Then sit right down in the rocking chair and hold him tight."

Rick snapped more pictures of the two of them as Andrea began to read, making the fairy tale come alive once more. When she'd finished, Tessa ran over and they cuddled for a long time while he got more pictures.

"I have some presents, too," he interjected. "One for you, Tessa, and one for Andrea."

He pulled the little packages out of his pocket. Rick started with Tessa first. "I didn't wrap this one because it's a present that was always yours, but I needed to wait for the right moment."

She took it from him, recognizing it immediately. "This is Mommy's ring."

"Yes. I gave that to her when I asked her to marry me. We both decided that one day we'd give it to you to remember her by. We'll keep it in my drawer and you can look at it and wear it whenever you want."

Tessa took it out of the box. "I love you, Daddy!"

"I love you. It's yours, sweetheart."

"What's your present for Andrea?"

"I don't know. Shall we see what I'm going to give her?"

"Yes, Daddy. Hurry!"

With a smile because she was so predictable, he handed it to the woman he loved, but Andrea's fingers were trembling. When she removed the paper and opened the velvet-lined box, she gasped.

"That diamond is the color of your eyes, Andrea. They're heavenly, just like you. I bought it a few days ago because there was no way I was ever going to let you go." He reached in and put it on her ring finger before he looked at Tessa. "Do you know what this means, sweetheart?"

His daughter was a quick study, because she said, "Did you ask her to marry you yet?"

Rick roared with laughter.

"He did." Andrea spoke for him with her eyes more dazzling than the blue diamond set in the gold band. "And I said *yes*."

"It means Andrea has consented to be my wife and your new mommy."

Her face lit up. "You're going to get married and live here with us forever?"

"That's the idea." He leaned between them to kiss Andrea long and hard in front of his cherub. "I love you," he whispered fiercely.

Andrea threw her arms around his neck. "I love you until it hurts, Rick. I'm not afraid anymore. My mother is going to be overjoyed, because she loves you, too. You've made a brand-new woman out of me. I'm going to take your love and run with it for as long as we're granted life, because you and Tessa *are* my life and this is just the beginning."

* * * * *

HARLEQUIN®

Romance

Available December 3, 2013

#4403 SECOND CHANCE WITH HER SOLDIER
Barbara Hannay

When Corporal Joe Madden returns to his estranged wife, Ellie, he wants her signature on the divorce papers. But stranded together in bad weather, could a Christmas truce bring the sparkle back into their marriage?

#4404 SNOWED IN WITH THE BILLIONAIRE
Caroline Anderson

Childhood sweethearts Georgia Beckett and Sebastian Corder are each other's refuge in a blizzard. Is it time to give their love a second chance?

#4405 CHRISTMAS AT THE CASTLE
Marion Lennox

When Angus Stuart offers Holly McIntosh the *temporary* position of chef in his castle, she's determined to make it permanent. Can she melt the Earl's brooding heart?

#4406 SNOWFLAKES AND SILVER LININGS
The Gingerbread Girls
Cara Colter

When Casey Caravetta meets Turner, her ex, at a Christmas wedding, it *doesn't* inspire much festive cheer. But maybe a little bit of holiday magic is just what they've been waiting for....

HRLPCNM1113

**Celebrate Christmas next month with Cara Colter's
Snowflakes and Silver Linings, the third and final story
in the sparkling Gingerbread Girls trilogy!**

Turner Kennedy had seen her as no one else ever had. But
she had seen him, too, felt she had known things about him.
Now, studying his face as he squinted up toward the porch
ceiling, she put her finger on what was different about him.

During those playful days, Turner Kennedy had seemed
hopeful and filled with confidence. He had told her about
losing his dad under very hard circumstances, but she had
been struck by a certain faith in himself to change all that was
bad about the world.

Now Casey was aware she was looking into the face of a
warrior—calm, strong, watchful. Ready.

And also, deeply weary. There was a hard-edged cynicism
about him that went deeper than cynical. It went to his soul.

Casey knew that just as she had known things about him
all those years ago. It was as if, with him, she arrived at a
different level of knowing with almost terrifying swiftness.

And the other thing she knew?

Turner Kennedy was ready to protect her with his life.

A second passed and then two, but they were long, drawn-
out seconds, as if time had come to an amazing standstill.

This was what chemicals did, she told herself dreamily. He
thought, apparently, they were in mortal danger.

She was bathing in the intoxicating closeness of him.

Casey could feel the strong beat of his heart through the thin fabric of his shirt. He was radiating a silky, sensual warmth, and she could feel the exact moment that his muscles began to uncoil. She observed the watchfulness drain from his expression, felt the thud of his heart quieting.

Finally, he looked away from the roof and gazed intently down at her.

Now that his mind had sounded some kind of all clear, he, too, seemed to be feeling the pure chemistry of their closeness. His breath caressed her face like the touch of a summer breeze. She could feel her own heart picking up tempo as his began to slow. His mouth dropped closer to hers.

The new her, the one who was going to be impervious to the chemistry of pure attraction, seemed to be sitting passively in the backseat instead of the driver's seat. Because instead of giving Turner a much-deserved shove—fight—or scooting out from under him—flight—she licked her lips, and watched his eyes darken and his lips drop even closer to hers.

Don't miss _Snowflakes and Silver Linings_, available December 2013—the third and final installment from the Gingerbread Girls!

HARLEQUIN®

Romance

Snowed In with the Billionaire
Caroline Anderson

One magical Christmas Eve…

Caught in a blizzard, Georgia Beckett is forced down
a narrow lane she'd hoped to avoid…and not just
because of the snow! The road takes her past the
beautiful abandoned house of her youth—the
new residence of her childhood sweetheart.
Sebastian Corder's shocked to hear the doorbell ring.
Is he ready to open the door to the past? But the
snow's getting heavier…and there's only one way
to find out!

Look for
SNOWED IN WITH THE BILLIONAIRE
by Caroline Anderson, coming next month
from Harlequin Romance!

Available wherever books and ebooks are sold.

HR74269